P.S. JANE

Jessica Julien

Desert Ink Press

Contents

To all the moms who never felt seen.

CHAPTER 1

Delicately slipping the last vibrator into the suitcase, and ensuring the lingerie and lube are secure, I zip up my merchandise with a satisfied smile. Standing the hot pink case upright, I straighten and begin organizing the receipts when thin arms squeeze me into a death lock.

It's three hours post party, and most of the women have gone home for the night to tell their husbands all about the salacious items they ordered, but the hostess lingers over me while I'm packing the goods. Being a pleasure party consultant has its perks, but one of the drawbacks is being embraced by boozy women. Being squeezed so tightly that I could pop like a can of biscuits, I stiffen.

"Thanks *soooo* much, Janie," Betty-Ann pipes. "I enjoyed this. So. Much. Fun!" Her voice reaches an ear-splitting octave that makes me wince.

Tonight was Betty-Ann's first time hosting a pleasure party. Known as one of the PTA's most "closed-up" women, I was shocked to find her engaged in the products and ordering way more items than I anticipated—more than any of the other women who attended the event. Now, she is wasted on my iconic boozy blend of Sprite Zero, Blue Curaçao, and Vodka that I mix for every party, and is smothering me like a pillow.

To escape her unwelcome hug, I force a smile and step out of arm's reach.

"So fun," I agree, tone bordering on sarcasm. It's a tone I can't help. After 248 parties and 248 hostesses giggling and teasing the merchandise, the *pleasure* part of the party has lost its sparkle for me.

I used to have a career in social work, but once my daughter Cheyanne was born, followed by Max a handful of years later, it was more important for me to stay home and care for them. I've never regretted being a stay-at-home mom, but once those little babes go off to school and no longer need 24/7 supervision, I was worried I would find myself utterly bored and stoic.

Which is how I found myself thrown into the world of pleasure.

I began working as a "pleasure" consultant two years ago as a way to help supplement our income until I found something better—a hobby of sorts. Selling sex toys... a hobby? Crazy, I know, but in the small town of Brightwood, where the population sits around 13,000 residents, it amazes me that, besides myself and one other woman, no one else has thought to indulge the bedroom secrets of the neighborhood wives. Any outsider—or neighbors of these women—would be shocked by how much money they spend on enhancing their nightly endeavors. Apparently, it's a huge market in this cozy town, and the job of ensuring those expeditions are fueled with fun rests on my shoulders.

Thus, the hobby became a *job*.

Now though, after my time as Jane: Pleasure Party Consultant, I've grown bored with the same routine. I admit, the income has been helpful the last year, covering added expenses for a needy teenage daughter and a growing boy. But the truth is, my husband, Peter, makes a decent salary as a professor at the local university and even without my income, we'd be okay. Which begs the question: Why do I choose to continue?

I guess it's only because it gives me something to do—some sort of meaning to being Jane McKenna (other than a mom). Plus, it's nice being able to say, "Yes, honey. You can buy that $40 lip gloss," when Cheyanne *needs* something important or Max wants to splurge on a rare comic.

So, I continue my legacy as the mom who sells dildos and edible underwear.

"Lemme ask you," Betty-Ann proceeds, words slurring together and interrupting my train of thought.

These after-party moments are not uncommon. Most hostesses trail me while I pack and get chatty, asking way too many personal questions as they graze whatever food is left out.

With an inward sigh, I watch Betty-Ann use a half-eaten tortilla chip as a wand, contemplating her question while chewing. Betty-Ann is petite, with short copper hair and brilliant green eyes. Tonight she's wearing a knee-length dress covered in daisies and a pearl necklace, something as iconic to her as my boozy beverage concoction is to me.

"What does your husband think 'bout *all* this?" She waves the chip toward the bedazzled luggage.

With a chuckle, I shrug. "He doesn't really want to know the details." Shoving my hands into my leggings' shallow pockets, I realize how tight their size sixteen is. Withdrawing my hands, I chastise myself for eating the second piece of chocolate cake. Then again, who can resist free cake? Not me!

Betty-Ann licks the salt from her lips as she leans toward me. My stomach churns as I watch this gross, slow gesture. "Do you two... you know?" She winks, lowering her voice. "Test the products?"

"Oh, Betty-Ann." I smirk, shuffling the receipts together and shoving them into my bag. "No." I cock my head. "Well, we don't make a habit of it at least."

Betty-Ann stumbles into a nearby chair with a heavy exhale. "I'm surprised he is okay with you doing this stuff." She sniffs, rubbing her nose like a toddler, then bursts into a fit of giggles. "Jackson heard the word *pleasure* and started squirming."

I smile because it's not an unusual response for spouses.

Betty-Ann tosses her head back, laughing deeply. "He called all his friends as soon as the date was set, wanting any excuse to not be around here tonight." Wiping a tear from the corner of her eyes, she gulps in a breath. "Then, when I suggested I might buy something..." Her eyebrows raise suggestively. "He's never been that shade of red before."

My chuckle is light. "Well, that's normal. Peter doesn't think much of it. Initially, he was surprised, but he's used to having all this around the house now."

"What do your kids think?"

As if I flaunt to my two kids that their mother sells sex toys in the late evenings on Friday and Saturday. I avert my gaze so she doesn't notice me rolling my eyes.

"We keep the merchandise in the garage, so..." I shrug again, zipping the last case closed, annoyed that people automatically believe I keep dildos and lube on the coffee table, as if they're conversation pieces on display. For some, maybe, but they aren't for me—not in my house anyway. I'm not the worst mom in the world. I do draw the line at public displays of sexy merchandise. I'm not about to be *that* mom in my kids' memoir of their childhood traumas.

Betty-Ann leans her elbows on the table. "You're one lucky lady." She blinks heavily, spinning one of her pearl earrings. "Have you ever thought about doing anything less..." Her eyes crinkle as she ponders.

"Salacious?" I suggest, and she nods. As I lean against the edge of the table, I think about how my life used to be. "Before I had Cheyanne, I worked in social services, but having kids changes a lot of things, as you know." Betty-Ann gives me a knowing smile, having one daughter of her own in seventh grade. "Two kids later and job opportunities change too. There aren't as many options—not in this town, anyway."

"Why don't you move?"

As if it were that simple. "Peter loves working at the university, and we love being part of this community. So, while I don't work in the social services field anymore, I work to keep relationship flames going around the neighborhood instead. Just a different kind of helpful service, I suppose." My tongue clicks sarcastically, but Betty-Ann is too busy covering a yawn to notice.

Pressing from the table, I lug my purse onto my shoulder, grab my luggage, and head toward the exit. It's not too late, and I want to get home and snuggle on the couch with a bar of dark chocolate and some wine. Suddenly, I feel very self-conscious about this job. Even though it's not the first time someone has questioned my hobby, tonight the concern hits me hard.

"So lucky," Betty-Ann repeats, standing to follow me to the door. She uses it to prop herself up as I leave, holding it open. "Thanks again, Janie. I had a blast."

I give her a parting smile.

"Let's get coffee next week," Betty-Ann perks.

My phone chimes in my purse. and I shuffle the bags to reach it. "Sure," I agree, not bothering to look back. We both know that we will not meet for coffee next week, let alone in fifty years. Despite every buzzed hostess's best intentions, those midnight promises have always disappeared in the morning. No one really wants to be seen out in public with me, especially the local coffee shops where most of the moms hang out during the day—the moms who've hosted parties, ones I know way too many intimate details about. It'll never happen, and that thought sinks into the pit of my stomach with an ominous weight.

Shoving the cases into the back of my van, I slide into the driver's seat. Finally, I find my phone and an email notification. Seeing it's from the CEO of the company I work with, I open it.

Hello Consultants,

Please tune in Monday at 7 a.m. PST for a very important announcement regarding the company and future changes we will be making. Use the link below to join the Zoom call, or tune in live on our Facebook page. If you cannot make the call, the recording will be posted on Facebook shortly after.

Thank you,

Beatrice Guntry, CEO

The ominous feeling in my gut solidifies like iron. This can't be good.

Standing in the dim kitchen, I pop the cork on a bottle of rosé. The house is quiet as everyone is in bed, but I relish this silence in the night. Taking a sip of wine, I sigh deeply. It hits my stomach in a wave of warmth and relaxation.

"Hey," a groggy voice says behind me. The sudden noise makes me jump and wine sloshes down my wrist.

I spin, seeing Peter sitting on a bar stool. He appeared as quiet as a ghost.

"Dammit, Peter," I exclaim, wiping the drops off. "You scared the hell out of me!" I try to calm my racing heart.

Behind his glasses, his mossy green eyes are half-closed as he yawns. "Sorry," he replies, "I wanted to see how the party went."

I lean my hip into the countertop, twisting the wine glass between my fingers. "It was fine. I made quite a few sales." As I take a sip, he nods.

"Told you these women would buy." He smirks, tapping his fingers against the counter.

"That new MD500 Vibrator was a hit." I snort into my wine glass. "You could never guess what Miss Prissy Patty ordered." I raise an eyebrow.

Although Patty is quiet and wears blouses buttoned to the neck, she has attended more parties than I can recall. Not that her clothing choices have anything to do with her bedroom needs, but she is known for her work with the church and shelters in town, not for her nightly activities. At parties, she sits in the back browsing the magazine, then orders something simple like perfume or bed sheet spray, but tonight was different. The items she selected even shocked me—it was my biggest sale of the night!

A polite chuckle escapes Peter's lips. "I can only imagine, but please, do *not* tell me," he adds with another laugh. "I don't need that mental image in my head every time she stops in to bring John his lunch."

Silence falls between us as I smile. The conversation with Betty-Ann replays in my head as I snap a piece of chocolate off.

"Does my job bother you?" I ask, popping the chocolate into my mouth. It immediately melts on my tongue.

"What?"

Rolling my eyes, I sigh. "Selling all this sex stuff… does it bother you?"

Peter hesitates, and I can tell he's thinking through his words before he speaks. "It's just a job, really." He lifts his shoulders in a shrug.

"Right. But does it *bother* you?" I reiterate. "Like when you're chatting with someone and they ask what your wife does… Do you get embarrassed telling them?"

He shakes his head to hide a smile. "You think I tell them, 'Oh, Jane? Yeah, she's in the sex industry!' No, honey," he bellows, "I inform them you host parties for women and they never inquire more. Well, not usually," he adds, scratching his jaw. "But your job is nothing to be ashamed of."

"I guess." I bite my bottom lip in thought. "Okay. It's just… we never talk about it—"

"Jane," Peter says, sliding from the stool and rounding the counter. As I nuzzle into his chest, I smell the familiar scent of blue sage, citrus, and sandalwood from his lingering cologne. "What you do doesn't bother me. I couldn't care less what the wives of this town do in their free time. Nor do I really *want* to know the details of their bedroom feats. But if what you do bothers *you*…" he says, lifting his brows, "you don't have to keep hosting parties."

"I know."

"The extra income is nice," he muses, placing a kiss on my forehead. "But you know we would get by without it."

"I know," I repeat with a bit of a grumble.

He draws away to look at my face. "Then what's the problem here?"

I stare into his eyes, pursing my lips. What *is* the problem?

With a shake of my head, I press a quick kiss to his lips. "Nothing, I guess. Betty-Ann just made a comment, and it got me thinking about my job and you and the kids…" I let my voice trail off.

"Jane," Peter says my name softly. "If your job bothered me at all, do you think I would ask to test that new MD1000?"

I giggle, pushing him away playfully. "It's the MD500, and I don't believe *you* would be the one enjoying it." I throw him a wink and nudge him. "Plus, Patty bought my last one."

Peter throws his head back and laughs. "Oof, I didn't see that coming." He runs his hands up and down my arms before kissing me tenderly. "Come on. Let's go to bed."

CHAPTER 2

"**G**ood morning," I sing, sliding a plate of toasted waffles across the counter.

In a heavy grunt, Cheyanne plops onto the barstool, muttering a reply. She reaches for the plate, but I hold the edge, forcing her to pause and look up.

"Good. Morning," I enunciate with a smile. Despite Cheyanne's attitude-loving tendencies, I'm not raising a rude teenager.

Cheyanne rolls her heavily lined green eyes. "Good morning."

My gaze wanders over her outfit as I release the plate. The sixteen-year-old daughter of mine is not afraid to flaunt her pear-shaped figure with a black and yellow striped top tucked into black high-waisted shorts. Shorts that are exposing quite a bit of skin.

"Are those long enough for school?" I nod, gesturing to her legs.

Flipping her long sandy ponytail over her shoulder, she glances at her outfit. "I've worn them before and never got in trouble." Cheyanne shrugs, adding syrup to her waffle.

I highly doubt they are long enough, but I know better than to start a fashion battle on a Monday morning. Letting the subject drop, I open my laptop to find the link for the meeting this morning. I don't want to miss whatever the important announcement is.

While I wait for the ancient computer to load, I turn my attention to

Max, a ten-year-old with a sweet tooth who is drowning his waffle with syrup. With a comic in his other hand, he gazes at the colorful pages as he pours.

"What are you reading this morning?"

"It's a Superman comic." Max takes an extra-large bite. Before chugging his orange juice, he swallows and wipes his mouth with his shirt-sleeve.

"Ick," Cheyanne squeals. "Use a napkin, *chimp*!"

Max sticks out his tongue before returning to his comic.

"Just eat your breakfast you two," I grimace, inhaling deeply as I chant, *Don't fight. Don't fight,* in my head. I slide a napkin to Max, then sign in to my profile on the computer. Seven minutes until the meeting begins. "Anything happening at school this week?"

"Nope," they answer in unison.

I narrow my eyes at them because there's never *nothing* happening during the school week.

"Who's the boyfriend of the week, Cheyanne?" I wonder, knowing Cheyanne flickers between crushes, as if changing the channel for better entertainment. Cheyanne and I are open about most subjects, and she is very much aware of what I do for work. She's seen the merchandise, asked questions, and we had *the talk* about sex after one of her friends mentioned what she overheard at her mother's party and what items were on display. Talk about an embarrassed teenager... and mother trying to explain what those *parties* were for. But I know she's only dating for fun and nothing more... for now, anyway.

Cheyanne groans, leaning back dramatically. "Ugh, *mawwwwm,*" she draws out the word. She rolls her eyes again, returning to her phone screen vibrating endlessly against the counter. "No one."

Taking a sip of my coffee, I give her a moment to respond to whoever she is texting. When she pauses to take a bite of her waffle, I push further. "What about that boy with the purple hair? Brad? Brendon?"

"His name was Brett, and no, I'm not seeing him anymore."

"Okay. So you're not seeing anyone?" I raise a single brow.

Cheyanne stuffs the last bite of her waffle into her mouth in order to avoid answering, but her shoulders rise and fall.

I huff, clicking open my email on the computer. My fingers tap in my password aggressively. "It would be *so* much easier if I could just read your damn minds."

Cheyanne glares at me as she reaches for her heavily creamed coffee, using the mug covered in holographic corgis to hide her annoyance.

"How cool would that be!" Max chimes.

"Uh, totally cool," I reply, finding the email from the CEO. Clicking the link, it opens a screen with a countdown to the meeting. Four more minutes.

"Can I have the car on Friday?"

My shoulders stiffen as I stare at Cheyanne, whose face is glowing from the phone and whatever social media she's scrolling. Seriously, why did I get her that damn thing?

As frustration rises within me, I instruct myself, yet again, to *not fight*. Before opening my mouth, I take a deep breath to ensure my tone doesn't sound shrill.

"You don't have a license."

She grumbles loudly. "Why won't you let me get it? It would make my life so much easier!"

"It wouldn't matter because I have a party this Friday and you can't take dad's truck because it's a stick shift." My voice stays mellow, but irritation and frustration mix making my pulse quicken.

Putting her purse on her shoulder, Cheyanne crosses her arms over her chest. With a stubborn stomp, her sandals clap against the floor. "Why can't you have a *normal* job?" She shouts. "Those are my friends' *parents*!"

"A normal job like..." I wait, fluttering a hand in the air.

Cheyanne throws her hands out in anger. "I don't know. A bank teller, a cashier, something less—"

"Scandalous?" Max offers, and Cheyanne shoots him a deadly glare. "What? I think what Mom does is cool."

With flushed cheeks, Cheyanne's voice rises. "You don't even know *what* she does!"

While Max may have an idea of what I do, hosting parties for women that involve bedroom things, we have yet to have a full discussion on sex and what all that "merchandise" in the garage is for. Eventually, he will either find out on his own, like Cheyanne, or I'll have to show him myself. But ten just seems way too young to be talking about vibrators and lingerie at elementary school. That is not a phone call I wish to receive from the principal.

"She sells toys, duh," Max replies, and he rolls his eyes.

Don't fight. I hold my breath. Counting to five, I wait for them to reach a point where I must intervene. Monday morning arguments are the worst.

Cheyanne snickers. "Yea, special s-e-x toys," she spells out, utterly disgusted.

I drop my head into my hands. The timer on the computer screen clicks down to two minutes. I do *not* have time for this!

Cheyanne is fuming. One of her hands is holding her phone while the other flings about like a weapon.

As Max slides out of his seat, he turns to his sister, hands on his hips. "I know what s-e-x spells. We watched a health video a few weeks ago." His gaze narrows in exact symmetry with my gesture. "I'm not five. I know things, Cheyanne." Max says her name in a mocking tone.

"No, you're ten, *chimp*." Cheyanne towers over her younger brother, reminding him who is in charge.

In my gut, irritation snaps like a rubber band.

"Enough!" I slap my palms against the counter to draw their attention. My finger points at Max. "You don't need to know that those letters go together for any sort of reason. Not yet, anyway. But we can talk about *that* later." My gesture swivels toward Cheyanne. "And you. Embarrassment can wait. I don't have time for this. I'm about to begin a meeting *for my job*." I fling my hands up. "There just isn't enough time in the damn day for all of this!"

"Mom," Cheyanne rebuttals with pursed lips.

"Just stop! You are not getting your license until you can show us you deserve it. Show us some responsibility for once. You're sixteen, dammit! Act like it!"

As Cheyanne opens her mouth to argue, I shoot her an icy glare, causing her to rethink what she's about to say. She clamps her lips into a tight seal.

One minute flashes on my screen.

"Get your backpacks. You're going to miss the bus," I say through my teeth.

Peter shuffles into the kitchen, buttoning his checkered shirt over his finely sculpted dad bod. "Morning, kids!" But they're already at the front door. "Bye, kids!"

After popping a coffee pod into the machine, he leans against the counter. "What was that about?" He withdraws his favorite mug from the dishwasher. A plain white background with two large poop emojis on both sides with the kids' names. "Dad's favorite turds" is written above them. A lovely Father's Day gift from four years ago.

"Just the normal morning drama." I shake my head and shift my computer to one barstool. The meeting should start any second now. I sip my luke-warm coffee, then exhale sharply.

"What's wrong?" Peter asks, pressing bread into the toaster.

I rub my hands down my face. "Just waiting for this meeting to start. Some big announcement."

His eyes light up. "Maybe they're promoting you all. Oh"—he snaps his fingers— "maybe they're starting a men's exclusive line. They finally got those letters I've been sending. About time!" He chuckles, and it makes me smile.

I set my mug down as the screen turns blue and a spinning circle appears, letting me know my host will be with me in a moment. "All your dreams are about to come true! Your husband can now host parties with you!"

"Hey!" he grins, pointing at me. "That rhymed." We share a laugh and then I quickly shush him as the screen fills with the image of the CEO. Suddenly, I feel clammy and unsettled. I have a horrible feeling whatever she's about to say is going to set off a lot of people.

Beatrice Guntry grins into her camera. She's in her fifties, but one would never know. Her blonde hair is freshly bleached. Botox has smoothed the wrinkles on her forehead and around her eyes and mouth, and her body is fit under the tight pink tank top she's wearing. I bet her boobs are fake, like most of her face, because no one at that age has breasts that perky poking out of their low cut tops.

"Hello consultants!" she exclaims. "Thank you, everyone, who took the time to be here live with me today. If you're watching this at a later time, I'm sure you've already heard the news, but please stay and watch the entire video for important information." Beatrice's voice is a dead giveaway of her age. There's a scratchiness to it, a subtle creak or coak in certain words, but still she's smiling her pearly whites.

Peter is quiet as he spreads peanut butter on his toast. He keeps eyeing me, waiting to see what's going on.

"The past twenty years have been wild and wonderful!" Beatrice says.

This is it. This is the announcement and already it sounds bad. My hands are shaking. Why is this making me so nervous? Whatever she says next won't *really* alter my life... right? This isn't a serious career meeting I'm sitting in.

"None of this would exist without all of you, my lovely consultants. But times do change, and we must change with them."

"Oof," Peter winces. Even he knows this is bad news.

I shush him, turning up the volume.

"With online markets, like Amazon, we have had a lot of big competitors to deal with. You've all been fantastic contractors, and this company will always have a special place in my heart."

Well, if that isn't hauntingly dim, I don't know what is, I think.

"But," she continues, folding her hands on the desk, "I'm sad to say that after twenty years of branding intimate toys and clothing, the company has decided to close the doors."

"What the hell!" I lean forward, squinting at the screen as if I didn't just hear what she said. The comment section floods with angry emojis and shocking remarks. I want to add my two cents about how unfair and sudden this is, but I decide to just sit back and see what else she has to say.

Beatrice nods as her eyes shift to the comments. Her head bobs as her eyes flicker left to right. The smile on her face has faded, but her light blue eyes still sparkle when they turn back to the camera. "I know you're all upset, and I promise to answer all the questions coming into the comment box, but know that this decision was not made lightly. As a company, we have to consider the financial future. Not just for ourselves, but for you all as well. After a lengthy discussion with our CFO, we all agreed that over the next six months we will stop all sales and hosting events 100 percent."

"Oh, no." I cover my mouth with my hand. Six months. Only six months to figure out what to do next. I glance at Peter. The pressure to be the sole provider and ensure we have enough money to cover any and all expenses isn't something I want Peter to shoulder himself.

So what will I do?

Find a new job? A new consultant agency? Go back to social work? I huff, running my fingers through my hair. My wedding ring catches on a tangle and I wince. All those options are possible... but where do I even begin?

"Now we have prepared a closing schedule—" Beatrice continues, but I can't even listen anymore. I slam the computer shut and slump onto the counter.

"Well, that's a shock," Peter says, licking peanut butter from his fingers.

I glance at him. "Six months." I sigh. "What will I do after they close?"

Peter shrugs. "There are other options out there."

"Like what?"

He ponders, sipping his coffee before answering. "You could start your own company."

I scoff. "Yeah, no thanks. I don't even know what kind of business I would start."

"You could work at the rec center or volunteer at the schools."

Straightening, I roll my eyes. "The last thing I want to do is be a receptionist. Not that there's anything wrong with it, but it's just not for me. And I volunteer enough with the PTA."

"You need a new hobby."

"One that pays."

Peter snaps his fingers. "Oh, take a pole dancing class."

I grimace. "Be serious." We share a chuckle, then let the silence hang between us.

"Why don't you and Lynn start something? Hasn't she always wanted to start a baking business or something?"

"Yeah, but..." I close my eyes. "I don't think she was actually serious about that."

My best friend Lynn is a wonderful baker. When she and her family moved here three years ago, we became instant best friends. Her husband, Andy, works at the university in the history department and, after a few staff meetings, became friends with Peter. It was only natural that when Lynn joined the PTA, realizing we both had sons in the same class, sassy attitudes, and an obsession with iced coffee, that we would immediately be forever friends.

More than once I've sampled her baked goods... okay, more than sampled. I've *devoured* them! And Lynn outsells every parent in any bake sale. Every. Single. Time. I've suggested to her many times that she could make bank selling her treats locally, but she always shrugs it off, not wanting to really discuss it further. Once, she seemed interested, but with talk of the financial start-up costs, the conversation dwindled like a blown-out candle.

Peter shrugs. "Never know until you ask her."

I nod, sucking in my lips as I think. After a moment, I run my hands down my face. "I guess I have some thinking to do."

Peter sets his mug in the sink and rounds the counter. Wrapping his arms around me, he kisses my cheek. "Jane, you have six months to figure it out, and we *will* figure it out. Just take the day to let it all sink in. Okay? No big decisions need to happen right this second."

"You're right," I admit with a sigh, tapping my fingers on the counter. "First things first is trying to get rid of all the dildos in the garage."

Peter snorts a laugh. "That would be an excellent place to begin."

CHAPTER 3

Tonight is party 249, and one of the few remaining parties I'll ever host. The thought of not lugging around all the merchandise actually makes me smile because yanking the cases up the two flights of stairs into Margret's house is killing my arms and back. I'm hoping tonight's party goes well and I can sell a lot of my inventory. The less I have, the less I have to figure out what to do with after.

This is Margret's third party. She is a well-known hostess around the PTA circle and loves opening her home to consultants. I believe she does it for the freebies as she rarely orders anything that will make her pay out of pocket, nevertheless, I'm grateful for her enthusiasm.

Her house is modest and clean, with wooden blocks tossed about the floor from her toddler. She apologizes about the mess as I unzip the suitcase, but I wave her off because honestly, her house is sparkling. Two of her kids run giggling, chasing each other with nerf guns.

"Aren't you going to say hi?" Margaret calls after them. The kids stop and back peddle. Troy and Tracy, twins that are a year above Max in school, give me a toothy smile. After a quick hello they're off again. "Sorry about them," she says to me.

"It's fine," I assure her. "Will they be going to a friend's tonight?" I have a strict no children policy, and I hesitate to even open my cases until they're gone.

Just then, the doorbell rings and the twins race down the stairs.

"Oh, yes. There's Nana now." Margret excuses herself.

When all the ladies have arrived, I turn the music down so Taylor Swift isn't overpowering my presentation.

"Hello, ladies! Welcome. My name is Jane, and we're about to have the best night." I select a product from the display on the table and hold it up. "Keep in mind, everything you *touch, tease, and taste* is discounted, so be sure to mark your favorites on the sheet provided, so at the end of the night, we know exactly what items to wrap up for you."

A few of the women share a giggle, while others hide behind their sheets seeing the first item I've lifted into the air. It's a lime green device with an assortment of buttons. Now, we begin the fun.

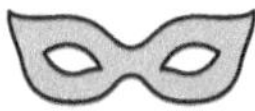

Four and a half hours later, I'm dumping my purse onto my kitchen counter. The party was an absolute bust! Not one woman complimented my token liquor mixture. Not that I make it for attention, but these ladies were more interested in discussing how many calories were in the *skinny wine* they were drinking instead. They barely touched my blue mix!

I grumble and glare at the half-filled pitcher I lugged onto the counter. Maybe if I stare hard enough, it'll just catch fire! Never in all the 249 parties had I brought home *leftover booze*! Unheard of!

Yanking the fridge open as if I have a vendetta against the chrome, I shove my arm in to find some ice and drop it into a tall glass. Filling the cup to the brim with my iconic beverage, I chug half in hopes of a fast buzz to drown the fury building within my gut. So far, it isn't working.

If anything, it only fuels it more.

Slamming the now empty glass on the counter, I exhale sharply. I didn't even make a single sale tonight. Not a *single* frickin' sale! Even after offering the hostess an extra 50 percent off an item and promising anyone who placed an order one freebie, no one jumped on the opportunity. I thought people liked free stuff? I like free stuff! Yet tonight, I couldn't even get a sale for some sample lube.

"Bitches," I mutter, filling my glass again. After chugging it, I repeat the process with aggressive angst. I'm pissed because I bought fancy vodka instead of the cheap stuff. I'm pissed I wasted gas driving there and back. I'm pissed I wasted my entire evening on those... those... "Bitches," I spit again.

Chugging the last few gulps in my cup, I decide I've had enough and dump the remaining beverage in the sink. I watch the blue mix swirl down the drain and then leave the sticky pitcher there, not even bothering to fill it with soapy water. Someone else can clean the dishes. I've had enough for today.

Stomping up the stairs like a toddler throwing a tantrum, I mutter, "Dumb fancy pants, women. Think they're better than me. Bitches. All of them. Bitches!"

When I enter my bedroom, I strip off my floral blouse and boot-cut jeans, then fumble through the closet for some pajamas.

"*Oh, that's too many calories, I couldn't possibly drink that,*" I mock in the best snooty voice I can muster. "*You want how much? Oh, sweetie. We'd never use that!*" I snort, tearing a t-shirt from the drawers.

Flopping onto the bed, I jerk the covers over myself. Peter is snoring. A loud, long snore of annoying thunder.

I side-eye him with a disgruntled glare, then close my eyes and breathe deeply. "If you aren't going to buy something, why book a party?" I complain.

Peter snorts and rolls over to face me. "Hey, honey." His voice is groggy. "How was the party?"

"Waste. Of. Time," I seethe, rolling to the edge of the bed and cocooning myself in the heavy comforter. "And I forgot to brush my damn teeth!" I toss the covers off and stomp into the bathroom. "Waste of time!" I snark and my words echo off the bathroom tile.

As I furiously scratch at my teeth with my toothbrush, I realize that the company closing in six months might be fine. Everything will be okay. If I had to continue handling women like this repeatedly, I may just go insane. It's about time I consider what I want out of my life besides selling goods. What more can I do? What will *thrill* me and fill me with joy every day?

With a huff, I drop my toothbrush into the cup and stare into the mirror. My eyes are tired and red and my hair is in need of a dye job, but I grip the counter and force myself to really take myself in.

"What is it you want, Jane McKenna?" After a moment, I realize my reflection is not going to give me the answers and my brain is too weary to compile a full thought. Instead, I make a mental note to sit down tomorrow and make a list of things I'm passionate about and move on from this shitty night. Jane McKenna may not be the pleasure party consultant of the town anymore, but she will be *something*.

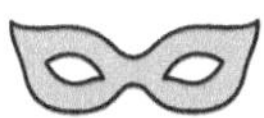

Letting the horrendous party from last night be the sign I was waiting for, I resolve to sit down with a notebook and make a list. Jotting down some bullet points could help me decide what I'd like to do or it won't.

At the ripe age of thirty-six, the last thing I want to do is sit in a classroom full of teenagers at the career center. Taking my phone, I find their website and notice they don't offer a lot of night courses or options for hybrid classes, plus the tuition… It is expensive! Even just the certification programs are too much. I went to college. Tuition and books were costly, and that was *years* ago. With inflation, prices are outrageous.

Sure, Peter's job provides our primary income, and we are doing okay financially, but this added cost could become too much. It may not be possible in the next few months once the parties stop.

I purse my lips and puff my cheeks as I click on the "Do you qualify for aid?" button. Filling out the short questionnaire is a waste of time because I indeed do *not* qualify for any sort of assistance.

Slamming the computer shut, I chug my coffee, not even taking a second to enjoy it. I sit in silence, staring at the empty cup as if a secret message was about to show itself in the few grounds on the bottom. Perhaps a recipe for sleeping in. Then I wouldn't fool myself into thinking I could change my life with a few clicks of a button.

With a yawn, I scratch off "career center" from my list and fix another k-cup. Maybe more caffeine will quell the ache of disappointment forming in my head. The low drone is turning into a pounding drum, and it's too early to deal with a headache. As I wait for the coffee to dribble out, I glance at the sink where the sticky, empty pitcher still sits. I flip on the hot water, squeeze in some soap, and let the container fill.

"Someone will get to you later," I tell the pitcher, as if it's hurt by being left yet again.

Everyone is still asleep, and I wouldn't give up the few moments of silence before they wake by doing mundane tasks. Chores will have to wait.

Taking my hot coffee, I return to my list. Nothing comes to mind right away, instead I savor the quiet, envying my family's ability to stay up late and sleep the day away. Even Peter can sleep in on his days off. But me? I can't recall a morning where I slept past eight. Not a single day goes by without a list of things to get done, errands to run, events to drop the kids off at... a mother's job is never done. No matter what time of day—or night—it is.

"Organization," I remark, adding to my list. "I'm great at organizing." Tapping the pen against my chin, I consider what else I'm good at besides taxiing everyone and everything across town. As most of the household tasks fall on my shoulders, I've had to learn to manage my time and prioritize what needs to be done first. Taking a sip of coffee, I wonder if, even after Cheyanne and Max are off at college or living on their own, I'll still wake up at six to pay bills and run errands for the family? Is this really the routine I want for the rest of my life?

After I add a few more items to my list, I glance at my phone. It's quarter after seven. Max is usually the first one up, hungry for the day to begin. I consider making breakfast for the family, but shrug it off and instead, withdraw the cereal boxes from the pantry.

"Today, they're on their own," I say to no one but myself, lining up the options. With a satisfied nod, I take my notebook and head to the living room to contemplate.

CHAPTER 4

Tonight, Cheyanne and Max are at Peter's parents for the night, so we order Chinese food and indulge. It isn't often we get a quiet evening with just the two of us, and it's a nice change in routine from our weekly spaghetti Saturday.

"How late do you think you'll be tonight?" Peter asks through a bite of broccoli.

I quickly chew the orange chicken in my mouth before answering. "Not too late. Kelly's hosted once before, and most of the ladies coming will be repeat clients. I can't imagine being out past midnight."

Peter lifts one shoulder while simultaneously shoveling an enormous bite of rice into his mouth. He chews a few times, washing it down with a beer. "That's okay. I'll catch up on some grading. Just text me when you're headed home so I can..." He clears his throat and leans forward. "Get in the zone," he whispers with a wink. "If you know what I mean." The chuckle that follows is deep and suggestive.

"Oh, I think I know." I lean toward him, meeting his lips over the take-out containers. His lips are sticky and the kiss tastes like sugar, orange, and soy sauce. Peter inches his hand forward, caressing my cheek. "Save it for tonight," I whisper, drawing away.

"You're such a tease," he jokes, watching as I saunter into the kitchen with my plate.

I blow him a kiss over my shoulder, set my plate in the sink, and head upstairs to prepare for party 250.

There's no time for a proper shower, so I spritz my hair with dry-shampoo and run my straightener over it. Half decent, but it'll do. I select my favorite black shirt from the closet. It has ruching on one side that hides my stomach when I sit down and makes me feel slim and sexy. Double bonus!

While I've never considered myself obese, after having two kids, no motivation to join a gym, and refusing to give up desserts, I'm what Tyra Banks would consider a very "plus-size" model. I've watched *America's Next Top Model*, I know what I'm talking about. My XXL shirt and size sixteen jeans would not cut it in the fashion world. Although, I see more and more women my size getting attention, which is fantastic! Go curvy women!

"Jane McKenna, you look fantastic," I chastise myself. "No one is going to be looking at *you* tonight. It's about the products. Selling goods." I give myself a reassuring nod, take one last deep breath, and head to the van.

Music helps lift my spirits, so as I back out of the driveway I blast Miranda Lambert's "Mama's Broken Heart", and belt the lines as loud as I can. Her soft country tone settles my nerves as I head to the last party I'll ever host.

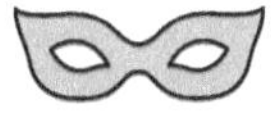

Before the party even begins, I've already tipped back two plastic cups worth of my boozy beverage. Miranda's tune is still cycling through my mind and I hum the melody. The itch to let loose settles into my joints and I relax. Already, the tipsiness sets in and I decide one more cup before the show will really give me enough buzz to get everyone going. Miranda's lyrics, "I numb the pain at the expense of my liver," trill over my tongue and I know I am on the right track to the perfect night.

The women surround the room, chatting and giggling. Hurriedly, I make my way around the space, introducing myself, handing each woman a cup filled with my iconic blue beverage. With a wide smile, I survey them, double checking everyone is holding a red plastic cup before I shuffle my playlist to an upbeat Taylor Swift song. When the voices behind me quiet, I know it's my cue to begin.

My eyes dance over every item in my open luggage case. I smile, withdrawing the newest device; one that will make the ladies shout in gleeful squeals and clap. Might as well start off with a bang tonight.

"Let's talk toys, ladies," I declare, spinning on my heels and almost toppling. No one notices though, because their wide eyes are glued to the extremely large silicone dildo waving about in my hand. Feeling balanced, I explain, "This is the DT250! Large and in charge, am I right?" I play off the energy in the room and the warmth buzzing through me. "It has ten—yes, *ten*—levels of pleasure."

"Ten?" a blonde woman gawks.

"Ten!" I raise my eyebrows in a dare-to-look-for-yourself fashion.

She blushes, but takes the product and examines it delicately, as if it might spring to life on its own. Honestly, if she wasn't careful, it would.

"Now, don't get too touchy, Bev, you sly dog." The words spill from my lips before I can stop them. I'm not normally someone who teases and jokes around in this way, but tonight I've thrown all my cares out the window and embraced the weird spinning feelings inside me. Tonight, I, Jane McKenna, will allow myself to drink the week away and let the confidence flood through me. I will let the women squeeze, touch, ogle, and rub as many items as I brought because eagerness and sex sell. At least that's how the saying goes, right?

I've heavily discounted the items in my cases and end up including one free item for any order placed. By the end of the night, my stock is low. Besides the displays I'll have to trash, almost everything is gone. As I load the receipts and magazines, I smile. Perhaps everything *will* work out for the better after all.

I stumble home well past one in the morning, dropping my purse on the floor and kicking off my flat. Shoving the frizzy hair out of my eyes, a few strands catch on my sticky fingers. I suppress a giggle as I try to free the locks from the mess.

Running my hands under cold water, I scrub the sugary mess left behind from the cookies and juice and booze and chips and everything else I ate at the party. A half-filled bottle of tequila was passed around at one point, and we all took turns pouring shots and biting into lime wedges. I used this opportunity to discuss lingerie and cup sizes to help sell the last few pieces from my case. *Cha-ching!*

While packing up, I locked my keys in the van, and then the ground seemed to ebb and flow beneath my feet. I called an Uber because I, for one, do not condone drinking and driving.

The clock in the living room ticks loudly against the silence. Gentle snores from Peter carry downstairs. The house is dark except for the dim hue that runs under the cupboards, but I don't bother turning any more lights on.

Exhaustion rolls over me and I fear if I lay my head on the counter, I'd fall asleep before I felt the cold against my cheek. Contemplating passing out on the couch or forcing myself to conquer the stairs undulating before me, my stomach growls. I swallow against a rough bitterness lingering at the back of my throat and decide a quick snack will help me decide.

Jerking open the fridge, I squint against the illumination. It takes a moment for me to comprehend the contents. I see milk and coffee creamer first. Hard pass. Anything with a creamy base will only make my stomach roll and heave more. Apple juice is a good choice for a quick swish. My teeth already feel fuzzy and gross and I need something to clear it before I puke. Withdrawing the juice jug, there's only enough for a single gulp. I toss it back on the shelf.

"Rude," I snark. Reaching past foil covered plates and a questionable looking Tupperware hoping to find some water, I come up empty-handed.

Just as I'm about to slam the fridge shut and stick my mouth under the faucet, I pause. A teal liquid in a tall cylinder catches my eye. With a shrug, I snatch it, pop the plastic top off, and take a whiff. The scent of berries and honey undertones rattle my senses.

"Oh, Gatorade. Perfect!"

I down the contents, then smack my lips together. It coated my tongue in a weird layer of slime and it makes me shudder. I gag, but thankfully, everything stays down.

Searching the container for an expiration date, hoping for all things good, I did not just drink an entire moldy sports drink; I come up short. Not only is there no date, but there's no label. My anxiety runs hot and sour in my gut because what the hell is this?

My stomach groans with displeasure, rolling fearfully. I drop the empty container on the floor and race to the bathroom. Covering my mouth,

I fumble down the dark hallway. The walls seem to shrink around me. I grapple at them with a gasp. My lungs struggle to fill and the little oxygen I can inhale is hot and thick. I can't satisfy the need to breathe.

The smooth wall brushes my shoulder, and I roll so my back is against it to support my weight. It feels slick and I stumble, almost falling. Sweat trickles down the back of my neck in icy droplets.

Unable to catch my breath, stars edge my vision, and everything is stifling hot. The hall is spinning and I feel unbalanced. My vision trembles and there's a tinge of static in the air. I can't feel my legs and my knees ram into the plush carpet. Grasping at the fibers, I attempt to hold my ground. Even though I plant my hands on the floor, I sense I am floating. Drifting through time and space as the room tilts and shatters into a sea of undulating waves of fuzz. The ground rolls in swells of gray and black that dissolve into a growing abyss.

A high pitch whine grows so loudly, I fear my eardrums will burst.

I want to shout for help, but my tightly shut jaw silences my command to scream. It refuses to move, cramping in a painful ache.

You're home. You're in a safe place, I tell myself, laying my forehead on the familiar carpet. It smells of fresh linen and cotton and earth.

Gripping my ears, I try to shut out the piercing octave, but the noise seems to come from within my head.

"Stop," I plead through my teeth in soft desperation. Hot tears trickle from my eyes, down my nose, to land on the worn carpet.

A bright light flashes, forcing my eyes closed. I'm not in control of my body as it topples over, but the carpet embraces me with its tickling faded fibers until there's nothing left but the darkness and me.

CHAPTER 5

The scent of dust and Febreeze tickle my nose, waking me from the deep sleep I'd fallen into. My body feels heavy, like I'm made of iron and impossible to move. Drool drips from my half-opened mouth, and I struggle to adjust my arm to wipe it away. Everything is stiff and achy like I have the flu running through every joint and muscle.

Forcing my heavy eyelids to open a crack, they take in the gray carpet. I trail my focus across the hall and up the wall where family photos hang.

Why am I lying in the hallway? I wonder, the memories from last night crest in my mind dizzily. *Oh, shit.*

"Jane?" Peter calls. His hurried footfalls pound down the stairs. "Did you pass out on the couch?" He chuckles.

With a groan, I roll onto my back and my clothes stick to my cold, clammy skin. The hall light flips on, and I shield my eyes from the scorching brightness.

"Ow," I croak, then cough because it feels like sandpaper lines my throat.

"Jane?" Peter gasps. "What the hell?" In an instant, he is kneeling beside me, hands brushing the matted hair on my forehead. "Are you okay?"

"Well," I begin with a raspy voice. My mouth feels like it's covered in cotton and I force myself to swallow the bit of saliva in my mouth.

"I think," I cough. "I may have drunk a little too much last night." A giggle escapes me, and I smile sheepishly. I half shrug, trying to play this awkward and embarrassing scenario off like it's not a big deal that I literally passed out in the hallway.

Peter takes my hand and I squeeze it, letting him haul my ass off the floor. He grunts with the effort and I shoot him a single dagger glare that fades swiftly because once I'm on my feet, sharp pain stabs through the top of my head. I wince, sucking in air through my teeth. I lock my fingers into a vise around his grip and feel his knuckles crack.

"Easy." Peter's tone is soothing and calm as he guides me to the bar stool. When I release his hand, he shakes it out, flexing his fingers. "I thought you were coming straight home after the party. I took a book to bed, but I must have passed out before you got home." His eyes search my face and then he's gripping my palm, turning it to feel for my rapid heartbeat.

I take a deep breath, puffing my cheeks as I exhale slowly. His brows draw in as he counts the beats against the seconds on his watch. When he places my hand on the counter, I stretch my arms out across it so my pounding head can lie on the cold surface.

"I'm sorry. The party wasn't supposed to go that late, but I ended up drinking with the ladies and time got away from us." When my cheek feels hot again, I ease my head up and slump against the chair. "I'm sorry I ruined our night. I know we had plans."

Using the back of his hand, Peter feels my forehead. His lips press into a straight line. "I won't lie and say I'm not disappointed, but it's okay. There are more weekends." He smiles, but it doesn't reach his eyes. "I'm more worried about your rapid pulse and fever."

I snort a laugh. "I'm not as apt as I used to be at downing that amount of booze. This hangover is wicked nasty."

Peter responds with a titter, and he relaxes as relief washes over his face. "We aren't as young as we used to be. I don't think our old hangover cure of Gatorade and double bacon cheeseburgers will help anymore."

"What was it your mom gave you that Christmas in college?"

"Chocolate milk and beef ramen." He chortles, and I laugh too. "But if you ask my dad for a hangover cure, he would say pickles and a cold shower."

"My mom would scoff at the idea of a hangover. And anyway, that all sounds disgusting. I *could* go for some cold Chinese food and a *hot* shower, though." Resting my forehead in my palms, I massage my temples until the pain subsides. "Besides, I had Gatorade last night, and it obviously did nothing for my agony."

Peter rounds the island and pops a mug under the coffee dispenser. *I wonder what happened. She hasn't drank like that since college.* I hear him mutter.

"What?" I ask, lifting my head.

Peter turns and shrugs. "I didn't say anything." *Now she's hearing things—*

"Hellloooo!" Max sings, bounding into the kitchen in Batman pajamas. "Can we have pancakes?" He jumps onto the seat beside me.

I wince at his boisterous voice. "You're back early."

"Grandma said we couldn't stay. There's a church thing she's helping with. She didn't even feed us before we left, which is insane!" Max huffs. "What grandma doesn't feed her grandkids before kicking them to the curb this early?" He rolls his eyes, stretching his arms across the counter dramatically.

Cheyanne sashays in, wearing leopard yoga pants and a simple black shirt. I watch as she makes a beeline for the stairs without a single glance in our direction.

"She *did* offer to make us breakfast, but you said you didn't want oatmeal," she remarks.

"It had *prunes* in it!"

"Raisins, *chimp*!"

Max makes a gagging sound before dropping his head onto the counter. "I *need* pancakes, dad. So, so, so many pancakes or I might just die." *And bacon,* I hear him add.

I brush back my staticky hair and smirk. "We don't have bacon, but we might have sausage in the freezer."

Max straightens, narrowing his gaze at me.

"What?"

He doesn't respond, but slides off his seat and takes measured steps to the freezer. I exchange a humorous glance with Peter at Max's odd charade.

"Hey, what's this?" Max bends to retrieve something by the fridge. He stands, holding the empty plastic container I dropped last night.

I wave him off. "A juice container. Can you toss it in recycling?"

Peter sets a steaming mug of coffee in front of me, then turns to see what Max is holding. His eyes bulge. "Where did you find this?" he blurts, snatching the container.

Max points to the floor, then opens the freezer in search of sausage.

"Shit!" Peter spits.

Max gasps, popping out of the burst of cold air. "Dad said a bad word!"

"Shit!" Peter repeats, dropping to his hands and knees to examine the floor. "Dammit. No! No, no, no!" His voice grows loud with panic. *Holy mother of all things... shit shit shit!*

I stand, stepping around the island to withdraw the griddle for pancakes. "Honey, stop. What are you freaking out about? It's just a juice container."

Peter pops up, turning on me with wide eyes. "This was *not juice*!" he exclaims. *Holy fuck!*

"Stop with the language," I demand, whipping a spatula at him.

"Who drank it?" His eyes dart between Max and me.

Max shakes his head, causing his fluffy bedhead to bounce.

"I told you and your sister not to touch this!" Peter slams the container on the counter, then runs his fingers through his short hair. *Fuck. Fuck. Fuckity fuck.*

I smack him softly with the spatula. "Cuss one more time in this kitchen, Peter, and I will have whatever God or Goddess is available smite you *right here and now*!"

Max giggles, but bites his lips closed when my wicked gaze lands on him. I wait for my words to settle, then lower my spatula weapon.

"The kids had nothing to do with it. They weren't even here last night," I tell Peter, spritzing the griddle with non-stick spray. "I drank it."

The confession hits Peter as if I slapped him across the face. He stumbles back a step, covering his mouth with his hand.

"You did *what*?" he shouts. *Shit. Shit. Shit!* "Tell me you *did not* drink this!" Peter rushes to me, clutching my free hand. His eyes dance over my face, looking for what, though, I've not a clue.

Cheyanne yawns, stepping into the kitchen with a messy bun and fresh lip gloss. "Why is everyone shouting? It's too early for this." *God, mom looks like shit.*

"Excuse me?" I push past Peter to wave my spatula at Cheyanne. "Mom looks like shit because mom stayed out too late and mom had too many damn drinks! Mom is a prime example of what you shouldn't do. Now or ever!" Using the spatula, I nudge her shoulder and her brows draw into a tight line.

She rolls her eyes. *Some role model.*

I gasp, taking a giant step back because as clearly as I heard her words, Cheyanne's mouth didn't move.

I'm dead. Fired. Fucking dead. I'm going to be buried alive. Fuckity fuck. Fuck. Fuck. Peter's voice rings through my mind and I spin to face him. His now pale face is staring at the floor, hands gripping the paltry amount of hair he has left, and continues to curse and spew profanities.

I cover my mouth. My heart races. Just like Cheyanne, his lips stayed closed.

Something weird is happening, Max sings.

"Yes, Max. Something weird *is* happening." I lower my trembling hand, and look at Max. He's staring at me in confusion.

Dammit all, Peter shouts. I pivot and whack him on the arm with the spatula.

"Ow! Stop that!"

"What was that thing?" I shout.

Peter licks his lower lip and takes a steady breath. "It... it was from the lab."

"From the lab?" I narrow my eyes.

His head bobs once and then he gulps. "The... uh, the research team I'm leading for th-the biochemistry department." His voice trembles. It takes everything in my power to stand still, because I want to shake the answer out of him. "It is... well," he continues. "That *was* the compound the facility sent us to examine."

My stomach twists into a knot. I feel the blood drain from my face.

"An experiment?" I seethe. "You left an *experiment* in our *refrigerator*?" I accuse through my teeth as calmly as possible, all while taking a dangerously slow step toward him. "The fridge where we keep our milk and eggs and *consumable* items?"

Peter's paralyzed, but his eyes flicker behind me where the kids are consuming this kitchen match like the next blockbuster film.

"This fridge," I motion toward the old, yet trusty, machine, "that any of us could reach in and I don't know..." I drop my hands to my thighs with a *thwack* that startles him. I even hear the kids take a collective, shuddering inhale. "Take it!" My voice is sharp, and I wave the spatula aggressively at him.

Peter gulps again. "Y-yes. That fridge."

"And I, your loving wife, drank it." I place the hand with my spatula over my heart and tilt my head. Leaning forward, I lower my voice. "I *drank* your experiment?" I enunciate the words, making sure each syllable digs into him like a jackhammer.

No one moves. No one speaks. Not even their unspoken words drift through my mind.

I inhale through my nose loudly. "I drank your experiment?" Everyone flinches when I shout.

Oh shit, Cheyanne gasps internally.

It's a rare occasion when Peter and I fight in front of the kids, or that we fight at all, but I knew this golden moment would forever be branded into my children's mind as the day their mother lost her damn shit and murdered their father.

Peter hesitates, but his head bobs once. "It would seem so. Yes."

I scowl with fuming indignation. The griddle behind me smokes, as the oil I had sprayed on is now burning. Any second, it'll send the alarms blaring. Already, the air stings the back of my throat as I breathe in the greasy oxygen. And yet, I don't move.

From the outside, I would imagine puffs of hot steam exhaling from my flared nostrils as if the sleeping dragon inside me has woken and is ready to ignite anything in my way. Right now, that is my *loving* husband.

"Uh, mom?" Cheyanne says hesitantly. I shift my eyes in her direction without moving my head. She gestures to the griddle.

I give her a curt nod and glare back at Peter. After an extended pause, I finally blink and break my hold on him. Peter exhales sharply, as if he'd been holding his breath this entire time. And he probably had been.

In one swift motion, my hands are free of the spatula and I've unplugged the griddle, dumping it into the sink with a loud sizzle. The hiss of steam on the hot pan expands into the silence until it too goes quiet.

Taking deep, calming breaths while staring at the murky sink water, I can feel Peter's uncertain gaze burning the back of my neck. He's watching me, waiting to see what I'll do next.

Good. Calming down is good. We all need to calm down. His voice quivers in my mind.

I clench the edge of the counter, my knuckles turning white. "I *am* calm."

Mom is losing it. Cheyanne's alto voice is querulous.

Rolling my neck, it pops a few times, releasing some tension before I respond. "I'm not losing it." I release my grip on the counter and spin on her. "It's fine. I'm fine. We are all fine." I clap my hands and force a smile that feels a little sardonic.

Lifting my attention, my family is gaping at me. Open-mouthed, shocked stare, what-the-fuck-is-happening gapes.

"What?" I blurt, startling them once more.

All three of them exchange looks of confusion and worry, but it's Max who speaks up.

"Um, mom? We didn't say anything." He lets the words linger, staring with a twinkle in his eyes, wanting me to understand... something.

I close my eyes, stretching my hands beside me. "I heard—"

"But we didn't *say* anything," Cheyanne interrupts.

Fluttering my eyes open, I look between my family members, wondering if this is all some drunken dream I'm having. I shake my hands out and will myself to wake up, but when I settle, nothing has changed.

Putting my hands on my hips, I face my husband head on. "Peter," I begin, my voice wary and soft. "What was that compound supposed to do, *exactly*?"

Peter wrings his hands together. "Um... well... we aren't sure yet. I just received the component and wanted to study it on my own before introducing it to other samples. That's why it's here... I was... preparing a game plan. Processing what I could. It's supposed to be kept quiet—not leave the lab, but I just—" He fiddles with his glasses.

"But," he adds quickly, noticing my mouth opening to prepare for a banshee scream of irritation. "They speculate part of the compound to have chromosome enhancing abilities. Some kind of potent," he pauses, licking his lips as his words formulate in his mind, "thing," he finishes, unable to gather himself. "To help the sick grow stronger. Cure cancer. Dissolve tumors. Grow... stuff." He flutters his hands about.

"Things. Stuff. Wow, dad. What kind of scientist are you?" Cheyanne scoffs.

Peter rubs the back of his neck. "I'm a bit put on the spot here. Forgive me, Cheyanne, for not mentioning the scientific wordage that has slipped my mind under these stressful circumstances."

Leaning my hip against the counter, I cross my arms over my chest. "And all those things and stuff inside this compound, if drank by—oh, I don't know, an average and potentially healthy woman—should do what?"

Peter lifts his shoulders, head swaying.

I step toward him. "Take a guess, *sweetie*." My voice drips with poisonous saccharine. I wait for him to respond, watching the sweat bead on his brow. He isn't looking at me, but through me, as if inside his mind he is far, far away. It's a look I've seen a hundred times when he is working in the lab trying to discover a solution to a difficult calculation.

Shit. I need tests. Blood tests and—

"Good." I flash him a tense grin. "Let's get those tests done, then."

His brows furrow. "I-I didn't say..." he stammers, glancing at the kids for help.

Cheyanne sets her phone down, actually *removes* it from her hands, which I thought impossible, and rests her arms on the counter. She's watching us as if we're acting out a high stake reality show while Max is sitting on the edge of his seat eagerly waiting on every single word.

"Mom," Max chirps.

I tilt my head to look at him.

On Friday, I ate a poptart in my bed.

Tossing my hands into the air, I grumble. "I've told you a thousand times not to eat *in your bed*!"

Max's grin widens, showing off his childish crooked teeth. His eyes dart from me to Peter, waiting for everything to click.

Peter snorts, then covers his mouth as I shoot daggers at him again.

"What?" I demand, because I don't understand what's happening.

"Mom." Max's voice is soft. "I think you can read minds."

I scoff. "That's insane."

Holy fuck!

"Cheyanne! Watch your language!" I point an accusatory finger at the closed-mouth teenager, who bursts into a fit of laughter.

"Oh. Em. Gee," Cheyanne guffaws. "It's totally true. I have to tell my friends." She moves to pick up her phone, but Peter lunges, snatching it before she can.

"Oh, no! You can't say anything. No one can say a word until we figure this all out."

Max is bouncing in his seat. "Mom has superpowers!" he whisper-screams.

I can't help but smile because deep down, something feels different. My mind is clear and the tension in my shoulders has vanished. Something has awakened within me and given me a sense of ease and bravery I've never felt before.

Taking a second to assess the new sensations fluttering through my body, because until now I haven't stopped arguing to realize my body is buzzing, I notice how alert my senses are. I silently thank the not-Gatorade for whatever the hell it did to me, because dammit if I don't feel super amazing right now.

CHAPTER 6

The rest of the day, Max trails me, firing questions like a machine gun, determined to discover any other abilities I may have. Using his comic books as reference, he points out each super—power by power—but so far, the only thing I've been able to accomplish is hearing everyone's endless stream of thoughts.

I wonder if Tony Stark could invent something to help... he trills, thumbing through an Avenger book. *Or enhance—*

"Honey," I begin calmly. This is not the first time I've had to say this next statement. "Tony Stark is not a real person."

Max faces me, opening his mouth as if to speak, but clamps it shut, deciding against it. His shoulders slump and he lets out a long breath.

Great, I think to myself. *I've hurt his feelings. Again.* I hold my breath, counting to five to see what his next thoughts are. His head tilts and then his gaze lands on the comic pages again.

But Dr. Strange...

I release the breath I'm holding, puffing my cheeks, and do my best to tune out the rest of his chatter by singing loudly in my head. Lyrics from Lorde ramble together, the line "let me live this fantasy" plays over and over. I bite my tongue to keep myself from giggling.

A fantasy.

That's exactly what this feels like. Never in my wildest imagination did I think I'd have superpowers, or that superheroes were real. They just can't be! Right?

Maybe this isn't real. Perhaps I'm in a coma and this is a dream world I've created. I pinch my arm, but nothing happens.

Wake up. Wake up. Wake up. I command my mind, tapping the pads of my fingers against the space between my brows. If I can activate my third eye, maybe it will open the door to this alternate reality so I can get back to my regular life.

I know nothing of chakras or if this is how you charge them. Activate them? I don't even know the proper terminology, but I caught a late-night documentary once and recall that the third eye controls awareness. I think. Anyway, right now I'll give anything a shot to stop the voices in my head.

So far, I haven't been able to turn it off, but I can focus on one voice at a time. It muddles out the other tones, so they sound more like a Charlie Brown adult in the background with no audible words. But the noise... there's a lot.

What the hell is she doing? Cheyanne huffs.

I can sense her eyes rolling so hard they'll probably fall out. Cheyanne has avoided me by locking herself in her room with the music turned up loudly, wanting to drown out her private thoughts. I don't blame her. At her age, I wouldn't have wanted my mom in my head, either.

"I'm trying to wake my third eye," I tell her, not glancing in her direction because I know she's glaring at me with fire in her eyes. It already burns through my skin like lava.

Get out of my head. She sneers, and I hear a frustrated scoff.

I open my eyes and look at her. "It's not like I can control this yet, Cheyanne." She slumps on the couch to sulk, arms crossed as she clicks the TV on. "But I'm trying."

"Whatever." Her nose crinkles and her brows draw tightly together.

Cheyanne lost her phone privilege for the time being, knowing the second she could get on social media she'd be tweeting, snapping, Instagramming, or whatever combination of things teenagers do to broadcast her "Supermom."

"You know I'm *trying,* right? It's just..." I bite my lower lip, wanting to choose my words carefully. I'm not trying to start a fight with her, but I need her to understand this wasn't a choice I made intentionally.

Cheyanne's shoulders relax at my tone, and she glances over the couch at me. *I know*, she says internally. "And that's not how you activate your third eye, mom," she chides, returning her attention to the TV.

"I promise you can have your phone back after dinner. We all just need to set some ground rules." I nod and shift to leave the room, but pause as Cheyanne's thoughts fill with a string of curses. I bite my tongue to hold in my scream because I want so badly to tell her to knock it off, to ground her, to tell her "Hello! This isn't happening to *you*, this is happening to your mother. The one and only vessel that brought you into this world and changed your shitty diapers. Me! Not you!" I keep humming and go to the study where Peter is.

Standing in the office doorway, I observe Peter rummaging through a book. His fingers scan the page, while his eyes dance across the lines. After a second, he shakes his head.

I clear my throat and Peter peeks at me before continuing to flip through the medical book.

"Find anything?"

Peter mutters something under his breath I can't make out, but I imagine it's not good. I wait, tapping my fingers against my thigh, listening to the string of confusing medical terms running through his mind. Finally, he flips the book shut and slumps against the seat. Removing his glasses, he rubs his tired eyes.

"I haven't found anything yet." He runs his hands down his face. Slipping on his glasses, he stares at me. "Can you come by the lab tomorrow? I want to run a few tests. Draw some blood."

I nod. "I'll bring lunch."

"Good. Good." Peter scratches his jaw. "How are you feeling?"

Lifting my shoulders in a shrug, I give him a half smile. "I feel fine. Great, actually. My body is buzzing, like I had too much coffee." I chuckle, because the feeling is a bit exhilarating. Like a thousand bees are racing through my veins and it's hard to sit still.

Peter's brows furrow. His gaze slips to the books as he taps his finger on the desk and then his lips purse, and he reaches for another volume of medical research. I watch him trill the pages, stopping to place a post-it note and write himself a note.

Perhaps if I can find the DNA strand... his internal voice begins and I tune him out because I know I won't understand his trail of thought.

"Isn't there someone who should know about this? Someone who can help run tests and research whatever it is you think is happening."

He glances at me and sighs. "If anyone found out what happened—" he shakes his head.

"Peter," I say, shoving my hands into my back pockets. "Isn't there a whole team at the university dedicated to this project?" He stares at me, unblinking, but his thoughts whisper into my mind of misunderstandings of delivery or lost packages. I shake my head. "You really think you can keep all this secret from not only a team of researchers but the company *paying* you to experiment with their compound?"

His cheeks flush and he averts his gaze. "A team of college students... a research company in another part of the world... it wouldn't be unheard of for an overseas delivery to be *mis*delivered."

I raise an eyebrow. "I would assume you had to sign for a package of this sort. Or at least *someone* in the main office or building. Do you really want to get someone else in trouble? And why did you bring it home in the first place? Isn't that against protocol or whatever?"

Tossing his hands up, he slumps in the seat. "I'll figure it out, Jane. Okay? Just—" he draws his hands down his face in exasperation. "I've made some mistakes. I thought I could bring it home to begin examining it, observing it in its original state to help the students jump start their plan. But I—" He presses his lips into a line, staring at the ceiling. "Just give me some time to think this all through."

"Fine." I chew on my bottom lip, observing him for another moment. "I'm going to get dinner started," I say and ease from the doorway.

"Okay," he mutters, not looking at me.

I turn and step out, but his voice stops me.

"Hey, Jane?"

"Yes?" I pivot to face him.

Peter tilts his head, holding my gaze. *God, I hope she's really okay,* he thinks, but he opens his mouth and says, "You'll tell me if anything feels off? Wrong? Bad?"

I give him a tight lip smile. "Of course."

And with a single nod, his eyes dip to the notes before him. I watch as he leans his elbows on the desk, eyes going back and forth across the pages as a frown overtakes his features. When mutters of experiments and research studies flood his thoughts, I slip from the doorway.

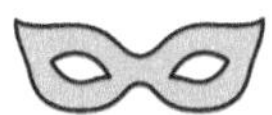

After the family goes to bed, I find myself unable to rest. My body itches to move, so I spend the better part of the night dusting, reorganizing, and wiping the inside of the cupboards. Who knows how long it's been since I did that?

Before I know it, the clock chimes 3 a.m. and a yawn escapes me. Finally, I decide to go to bed.

Once tucked in, I close my eyes, but in an instant they're wide-open again. A rush of energy surges through me, mixed with panic. How long had I been asleep? Rolling over, the clock blinks 5:30 a.m.

"What?" I whisper, as if the clock can actually respond and explain why I'm so awake so early. I've only been asleep for a few hours. How can I feel so rested?

Flipping onto my back, I squish my eyes closed and try to coax myself back to sleep, but they refuse to comply. I press my hands into my eyes and groan. Giving into the wakefulness, I slip from the bed. Since it's so early, I have time to shower before breakfast and I take full advantage. I wash my hair and shave my legs all in one go. I have not been able to do that at the same time in a long time.

Freshly scrubbed and smelling of lilac and orange, I head to the kitchen, humming an upbeat tune. I haven't felt productive before seven in the morning in years. I like it!

Lunches are packed, and I made breakfast before any sounds greet me from upstairs. As I'm withdrawing the last waffle from the machine, Max hops down the steps.

"Good morning," I chirp, sliding a plate of food to him.

Oh, score, he cheers, pouring syrup into every crevice. "Thanks, Supermom!"

I can't help but smile because I am *killing* this mom thing today.

"Where's your sister?"

Max shrugs, shoving a massive bite into his mouth. *Who cares,* he remarks, but I ignore it, focusing my mind elsewhere.

Closing my eyes, I shift my internal attention from Max's squealing and search the space for another voice. It takes a lot of time, but soon enough, Max's voice fades and another whisper eases into my mind. A frustrated grumble bellows through my thoughts. I wince, breaking my concentration, which causes Max's voice to grow louder, overlapping with what I assume is Cheyanne's irritation.

Piece of shit bra, Cheyanne snaps.

Waffles, waffles, I love waffles, Max sings at the same time.

Peeking at him with one eye, I see Max wiggling in his seat while chewing happily.

I take a calming breath and try the process again. There's probably a better way to do this, but it's not like I have any mentors I can ask for help. Instead, I visually shove Max's voice out of my head and listen to what other sounds I can pick up. After a few deep breaths, Cheyanne's commentary drifts back through my mind.

Piece of shit shirt, she continues, and I imagine her tossing clothes around the room.

Syrup. syrup. Oh, how I love you! Max's song chimes in the background like quiet elevator music.

I shake my head, willing Max's waffle song to silence itself, but I'm jolted when Cheyanne throws herself onto the barstool. I had been so focused on their jumbled thoughts, I didn't hear her come down the stairs.

"Everything okay?" I look at Cheyanne, taking in her outfit. A pair of dark skinny jeans and simple blue tie-dyed t-shirt. She looks cute and as if she'd tossed the outfit together without a second thought. Her long hair is woven into a fishtail braid and a few loose strands curl around her jaw.

Cheyanne glares her kohl-lined eyes at me, then scoffs like I'm some pathetic lowlife asking to hangout. I raise my eyebrows, inclining her to try that look again.

After a beat, Cheyanne deflates against the chair. Her grimace drops into boredom as she picks at the waffle before her.

"You know," I begin, leaning my hip against the counter. "If you need new clothes, you just have to ask."

"*Mom,*" she gapes. "Stay out of my head!" *No privacy, ever! I should just move out. This is so unfair!*

I turn and withdraw two cups, speaking to her as I fill them with orange juice. "You're not moving out, and you know I can't control all this yet."

Setting the glasses before them, my gaze connects with Cheyanne's fury. It's a look I recognize as one of my own she's picked up during her adolescence. The kids call it my stink eye. It's a look that draws the truth from them when items were discovered broken, or when one told on the other.

"Look." I sigh, resting my elbows on the counter so I'm eye-level with her. "I promise to try to not listen to your thoughts, okay? That's the best I can offer for now. But I'm trying. I really am."

Cheyanne takes her cup and winkles her nose. *Fine,* she thinks, and I nod in acknowledgement.

"I think it's awesome!" Max hollers. "What am I thinking right now?"

I smile, scratching my chin and trying to concentrate on his sporadic thoughts. "You wish you had some bacon to go with your waffles. And... the number seventeen."

Max applauds, and I bow my head.

Pressing from the counter, I reach for my coffee cup. "How about we go to the mall this weekend, Cheyanne? Just you and me."

Cheyanne blinks. "Really?" One eyebrow flickers up. I'm not sure if this facade means she's interested or thinks I'm totally insane for the offer.

"I could use a few new things. It might be fun."

You could use a new wardrobe, she remarks. "How about I just take the car and go myself? I can pick you out a few things."

My head sways. "Not a chance."

"Then no thank you."

"Cheyanne, really?"

She shoots me an arrogant smirk. "The last thing I want to do is go shopping with my *mom*. What am I, twelve? Besides, ordering online is way easier."

Don't comment, I tell myself, then turn to busy my hands before I react with some witty remark. In a single swoop, I grab the sack lunches I prepared and spiral back to plop them before the kids. Max and Cheyanne exchange a weird look, then her gaze pivots around the kitchen, taking in the sparkling countertops, dust free shelves, and mopped floor.

"Mom? How long have you been awake?" Cheyanne asks.

I click my tongue at her in annoyance. A clean house doesn't deserve an interrogation. Since when is it wrong for a mother to pack her kids a lunch for school? Although, it has probably been years since I've done more than throw an Uncrustable and an apple in a plastic bag and stuffed it into their backpacks.

"A while," I state, moving to open the dishwasher that's waiting to be unloaded.

"Something smells good," Peter calls cheerfully. Stepping beside me, he places a kiss on my cheek, then begins his morning battle with the Keurig.

"Mom's been binge-cleaning," Cheyanne accuses, as if our house has never been clean before.

"And she made us all lunch!" Max snatches his bag and peeks inside. "Not just Cup O' Noodles either, a *real* sandwich, and food! And look… fresh waffles. Not frozen!"

I press my lips into a line and stare at the ceiling. *Don't snap.* "I'm fine," I claim, withdrawing a dinner plate from the dishwasher. It's still warm, but the burn feels oddly soothing.

That's strange, I hear Peter think.

"Not strange."

Mom's probably got a parasite growing inside—

"I said I'm fine," I snap, my voice cracking the air like lightning.

Everyone gasps, and the room falls silent. The plate in my hand shatters, crumbling to the ground in tiny pieces. These plates are thick enough to be a weapon. In all the years we've had them, we've never broken a single one. Yet, here I am, standing with the pieces between my hands.

"Honey? Are you okay?" Peter's voice is whisper soft.

"Open the trash can, please."

Peter doesn't move. His eyes glance between the plate and the kids. Worry shadows his face. "Jane," he says my name in a disgustingly charming manner. What does he think? That I'm on the edge of a building telling him I believe I can fly?

My jaw clenches. "The trash can. Please." This time, he steps forward, careful not to step on any sharp pieces, and opens the cupboard under the sink. I deposit the shards. As I straighten, I realize Cheyanne is behind me, holding the boom, wide-eyed and cautious.

No one speaks as I sweep, and I do my best to ignore their worried remarks in their heads. No one moves as I run my hands under cold water. It's as if time has frozen and I'm the only one able to shift through it.

When the mess is clean, I turn, grabbing Peter's now filled coffee mug from under the machine, and paint a smile on my face.

"Everything. Is. Fine." I sense everyone holding their breath. Taking my time, I meet eyes with each family member, then shift back to the dishwasher. I continue unloading the cups, setting each one on the counter with a soft *clink.*

I wish dad would say something, Cheyanne states. *Clink.*

This is awkward, Max sighs. *Clink.*

I can't even... no, stop. She said she's fine. She's fine, Peter tells himself over and over. *Clink.*

"So what if I've been cleaning a bit... excessively," I tell them, placing the cups in the cupboard now. "I got two, maybe two and half hours of sleep last night and I have a lot of energy today." The silverware is next, and I toss them into the drawer unceremoniously. "I'm just using it all to get through my never-ending to-do list. That's not a crime. That's not weird." An awkward, almost maniacal, chuckle escapes me and I bite my tongue.

Two hours of sleep? Peter thinks, bewildered.

"I'm halfway through that to-do list, if any of you care. If not a bit more." I feel like I'm talking to myself; reassuring myself that it really is all *fine.*

The dishwasher is empty, and I move to the sink to load the few dishes into it.

"I think I'll tackle the rain gutters next," I continue. "Maybe check the attic for leaks before the rainy season." All the dishes are loaded, so I close the machine, dry my hands, and lean my back against the counter. I snap my fingers. "Oh, I was thinking we'd plant some tomatoes. The neighbors gave us a few starters. I don't think they're dead yet."

Peter rubs the back of his neck. "Plant... tomatoes?" he asks, puzzled.

"But, why?"

I shrug. "It's not like we wouldn't use fresh tomatoes. You like them on sandwiches and the kids like salsa—"

We could make spaghetti sauce! Like on TV, Max thinks.

"Of course we can. Great idea!"

Peter cocks his head. "Jane, you don't even like salsa." He raises his mug to me as if cheering this odd bit of inspiration, but his laughter turns into an unstoppable spew of giggles. "Tomatoes. Gutters. Jane, come on."

Max snorts, joining in on the fit of giggles. It only takes a moment more before Cheyanne musters whatever laughter she has within her and weaves herself in the eruption of hysteria.

I try to contain my own bubbling glee, but it fails.

This is all so weird, Peter comments.

This is the best morning ever! Max babbles.

My family is insane. How am I the only normal one around here? Cheyanne adds.

"Cheyanne, you are just as weird as us, you know," I say to her, wiping the tears from my eyes. We all settle, catching our breath, until I realize what time it is. "Crap. You're going to miss the bus!" I shove their lunches toward them and shoo them out the door. "And Cheyanne," I say, holding her back for a second. "Please, remember, we have to keep this all a secret."

"Yes, because I want my friends to think my sex-toy-selling mom has actually lost it and thinks she has superpowers." Cheyanne rolls her eyes, then folds her arms across her chest.

"Cheyanne..."

She sighs. "I'm not going to say anything, Mom." And then she turns and walks away. I watch them exit the house before going back into the kitchen.

I give Peter a kiss on the cheek and he wraps his arms around me.

"I haven't laughed that hard in a long time."

Peter chuckles, then kisses my forehead. "Me either." He holds me for a moment longer, then releases me to finish his coffee. "Don't forget you're coming to the lab today."

"I know. I'll be there right after the bake sale at Max's school."

CHAPTER 7

I pour my extra energy into baking for the elementary school fundraiser. Nothing from scratch, but box mix is better than buying the day-old supply like usual. There's nothing wrong with being *that* mom, because, really, I get it. Been there, done that more times than I'd like to admit, but I know showing up with freshly baked goods will put a twist in the PTA president's silk panties. Not that I actually know what she wears—or doesn't wear—but I assume someone like *her* would spend big bucks on *silk* undergarments. The idea of whatever she wears being knotted and uncomfortable makes me thrilled because Rebecca is a total stuck-up bitch.

As I make my way toward the plastic covered tables with fresh fudge brownies, blueberry muffins, and a dozen sugar cookies, I notice only a few parents have arrived. I'm not the last one, that's a first!

Rebecca's nasal voice carries over the path, and I cringe. I take a deep breath and remember that this is for the kids.

"You got this, Jane," I tell myself and continue forward.

"Jane!" Rebecca's loud voice is sandpaper against my ears. "You made it." She smiles a wickedly wide grin, folding her hands before her. Wearing pressed black slacks and a silk button down, Rebecca is the most sophisticatedly dressed parent here. "You brought baked goods. How nice." Her dark eyes roam over the containers in my hand.

I lift the trays with a triumphant smirk. "I did. Homemade and all."

"Wow," Rebecca feigns amusement. "Good for you for finding time." Her tone is barbed, oozing with sarcasm. *First time for everything, I suppose,* she thinks.

I click my tongue at her remark. "Yes, well, I would have Primed myself some fresh cupcakes, but they were sold out." I shrug. "It would have taken at least seven business days for them to arrive."

Rebecca folds her arms across her chest. "You can't Prime yourself *fresh* cupcakes." *This bitch...*

I take a step toward her and place a hand on her shoulder. "Oh, Becca." I shake my head and *tsk*. "You can Prime yourself *anything*." Stepping back, I set the platters on the table. "You should really try it sometime. So convenient."

She scoffs.

"There's a first time for everything, right?"

I sense her shocked glare on the back of my head. Rebecca's name-brand kitten heels tap in annoyance. A smile tugs at my lips, but I refuse to look at her, so I uncover the desserts and arrange them on the table.

"Today I'm mastering the bake sale," I tell Rebecca, then turn to face her. "Perhaps tomorrow I'll be running the PTA. Who knows!" I give her a rueful smile.

Rebecca's jaw clenches, and I imagine her perfectly straight teeth grinding behind the blood colored lipstick. *As if,* she thinks in a threatening tenor. With a huff, she pivots and stomps away. Her clacking shoes fade, leaving the rest of the PTA parents gaping after her.

"What was that about?" Lynn asks, appearing beside me. She's already unpacking her signature cheesecake brownies. Just the sight of them makes me salivate.

I'm so thankful Lynn joined the PTA because we became instant friends, bonding over Starbucks coffee flavors and gossiping about how annoying certain parents were. Other than her, I don't associate with the other parents. I can feel their judgmental stares on me, or the embarrassment from the ones who were recently at parties. As if I'd greet them and ask how their new vibrator is working in front of all the parents!

I beam, nudging Lynn's shoulder. "I think Rebecca is worried our homemade brownies are going to sell better than her pecan cookies."

Lynn rolls her dark, almond-shaped eyes. "Who brings *nut* cookies to an elementary school? Doesn't she know how many kids have nut allergies?" She shakes her head, then notices my trays of goodies. "Did you make these?" Snatching one, she stuffs a bite into her mouth. "These are great!"

"Yes, I made them. Is that so hard to believe?"

Lynn pauses, tipping her head side to side, making her gently curled hair sway with the motion. "Well," she swallows, "kind of."

I smack her arm playfully.

"I'm sorry." Lynn chortles. "You're just not known for your baking skills." *But damn, these are good. I hope not better than mine.*

"Uh, they're definitely not better than yours. Trust me." I take one of her cheesecake brownies and break off a bite. "I mean seriously, how do you make them so chewy? It's like an orgasm in my mouth."

Lynn smiles warily. "Yes, I—" She squints at me, then blinks a few times, brushing off the fact I just answered her internal dialogue. "Never mind. We have moms to outsell here."

The bake sale was a tremendous success. Lynn's brownies were the first to sell out, followed by the candy cookies from Betty-Ann, and then my sugar cookies! While cleaning up, I notice Rebecca shoveling the leftover pecan cookies into her tote bag with a vengeance, muttering under her breath.

Tossing my empty trays into the trash, I practically skip to the minivan, ready to tell Peter all about today's gossip and how I outsold Rebecca for the first time.

My cookies are delicious. I don't care what these parents say! I hear Rebecca's commentary as I pass. I slow, listening to her rant because her tone has a subtle hint of sadness in it. With a frown, I glance in her direction. Rebecca may be the biggest bitch on the PTA, but she does have feelings, too... I guess.

"Hey, Rebecca," I call and she sneers at me. "Those cookies are great, but maybe next time you should think about something without nuts." Rebecca's dark eyes narrow. "You know... allergies and such."

Rebecca doesn't answer me, but her lips curl into a wicked snarl before she pivots on her kitten heels and storms away.

"Okay. Good talk," I say, waving as she tears down the bake-sale sign. Why do I even bother trying with her? It's the same thing every single time. Show a little compassion or care and Rebecca snaps her pearly whites as if a kind word is actually a threat to steal from her pecan hoard.

At one time, Rebecca and I were actually friends—if anyone can believe that. When I first started with the PTA, I volunteered to help with the talent show and she was a kind of mentor, a guide to navigate the deadly pool of parents fighting for their child to be in the spotlight. Everyone thinks their child is the *best*. What kind of parents would any of us be if we didn't at least pretend our kids poop gold and are not goblins stealing our energy? Horrible ones, that's what! Shockingly, Rebecca was patient and understanding of every parent's complaint. I thought she was great and it made me excited to be part of more activities, but soon, something changed. Over the years she became cold and distant. Hateful and... well, bitchy.

I shake off the reminder of our *almost* friendship because the Rebecca I know now doesn't do *friends.* She only deals with peasants under her PTA dominion, squishing the small hope any of us parents have for the future of the children under her stilettos. With a huff, I slip into my van and let the memories go.

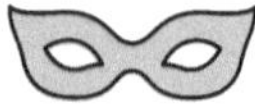

When I arrive at the University, I park in the visitor's parking lot and walk the winding trail to the science building. I pass hoards of students rushing from class to class and a few lingering on benches or smoking under the trees. As I stroll, I use this time to practice tuning in and out of conversations. I've done an okay job switching from person to person, but all the voices are still there in the background muddling through.

The bell tower chimes once, drawing me from my focus. I hurry down the path and into the old brick building. Three flights up, I find Peter in his office behind crooked stacks of papers and dusty bookshelves.

"Doesn't this place ever get cleaned?" I tease, stepping into the doorway.

Peter jumps at my voice, but noticing me, smiles. "Only when I have time."

While we eat our sub sandwiches, I fill Peter in on the bake sale. He half-listens, eyes flickering to the computer screen or the surrounding papers, but I don't mind because I can hear his thoughts running about the tests we're about to do and exam papers he needs to grade.

Tossing the wrappers into the trash, I brush my hands together. "So, what tests do we need to get done?"

Peter rubs the back of his neck. "We need to take some blood samples."

"I'm guessing we shouldn't do that here?"

His head sways. "We can use the lab. No one needs it until three today."

We head down a flight of steps to the locked lab. The room is chilly and smells of bleach and I shudder.

"Sorry, we keep it kind of cool in here for the chemicals," Peter apologizes, grabbing a lab coat off a hook beside the door.

"It's fine." I shrug, taking a seat at one table. The stool is ice cold, making me shiver again. "Let's just get this over with."

With a curt nod, Peter collects items from the shelves and arranges them on a tray. Once satisfied, he retrieved a clipboard and a fresh notebook from his desk and wheels a stool close to me.

"I'm going to start with just your vitals," he explains. I sit patiently, allowing him to strap blood pressure cuffs and other odd devices on my arm or wrist or finger. Finally, he pulls on a clean set of gloves and takes out a sterile needle pack.

Peter clears his throat. "I need to draw some blood."

"Uh, are you qualified to do that?" I eye the needle. Peter isn't a doctor or a nurse by any means.

He sighs, setting down the supplies. "I can do a simple blood draw." *Even though I've only ever done two in my life.*

I draw away, covering my exposed arm. "Excuse me," I snark. "You've only ever done this *two* times and you believe that qualifies you to stab your wife and hope to collect my blood?"

"Jane," Peter says, hanging his head.

"Don't *Jane* me." His jaw ticks at my tone. "Didn't you tell someone about this? Someone who can help you do these tests and run the samples?"

No. "I uh—"

"Don't try to cover up the fact that you haven't. I can read your mind, remember?"

Peter removes his gloves and runs a hand over the back of his neck.

"I would imagine there's someone—"

"Fine," he interrupts, shoving his stool back. He wheels away, stands, and stomps toward the door. "I'll be right back."

When he disappears and the door eases shut, I set my elbows onto the table. As they connect with the metal slab, an echoing *thunk* jolts me. I ease my arms up. The table has two dimples perfectly fitting the shape of my elbows sitting under the fluorescent lights.

"What the—"

"Did you just..." Peter's voice fills the room and I stand, spinning to face him. His eyes are wide, staring at the place on the table where it's bent.

"Did *she* just do that?" Another voice echoes Peter's and a figure shoves past him, crossing the room in hurried steps. Long, tan fingers examine the indents before he faces Peter again. "What is going on here?"

Peter's gaze bounces between me and whoever this guy is. I take a second to assess him. Tall, lean legs, fitted button down, and a mess of ebony curls tickling his ears. I've never met this man before, but a familiar university lanyard and ID tag hangs around his neck.

"Was this you?" Peter wonders, stepping close to peer at the table.

I gulp, rubbing my elbow. It doesn't hurt, nor did I feel pain when I made the connection. "Um... yes. I-I did that."

Peter scratches his jaw, then jots some notes. "Okay, well. That is new."

My head sways. "I guess I have more strength?" I say as a question, followed by an awkward chuckle.

"New?" the stranger spits. *What the fuck is going on!* His thoughts fill my mind.

"I told you about the compound we were receiving," Peter begins and the man nods. "It was said to have chromosomal enhancing properties." Again, the man's head bobs. "We weren't set to begin human trials for some time but—"

Oh, fuck. The man covers his mouth, stepping back. "Peter... tell me you didn't?" His dark eyes land on me.

"Hi," I say, giving him a small wave. "I'm Jane, Peter's wife, and accidental human trial number one." With a shrug, I extend my hand to him.

This can't be happening, he thinks, easing his palm to mine. I grip his hand, shake it and smile.

"Unfortunately, this is really happening."

"How did she—"

"Jane," Peter says, clearing his throat. "This is Professor Noah Chandra, Clinical Medicine. He's been invited to be part of the research team to oversee any testing on animals or humans." Peter pauses, giving a curt nod to Noah, then narrows his gaze on me. "Did you feel any kind of power build up when you slammed your arm into the table?" He wipes his wire-rimmed glasses, placing them back on his nose and focusing on his notebook.

"First, I didn't *slam* my arm down. I simply *plopped* it onto the table," I explain calmly. Peter glances at me for a second. "Second, no. There was no power surge. I just," I pause, gesturing to the table, "set my arm down like I normally would."

"Right," he muses, reaching for his notebook. After a few seconds of writing, Peter sets the note aside and rolls the tray with the blood draw equipment nearby. "Noah?"

The professor blinks at me, mouth ajar. His mind is spinning with questions and uncertainty.

I gesture to the table where the needle is waiting. "I assume you know how to do this?"

Finally, he tears his gaze away from me. "I'm sorry Mrs. McKenna, I'm a little—" he coughs, rubbing at his chest. "Can someone please explain, *exactly*, what is happening right now?"

"Jane drank the compound." At Peter's comment, Noah's eyes bulge. "And she is experiencing some... adverse side-effects."

I scoff. "If reading minds and extra strength qualify as *adverse*."

"Reading minds," Noah repeats softly. He staggers back, running his fingers through his hair tousling it more than it already was. *What the fuck!*

"We weren't set for human trials for some time, but..." Peter gestures to me. "I need your help."

We have to tell someone. Noah thinks, paling.

"Precisely what I've been telling him," I say, tossing my hands into the air.

Noah gapes at me, blinking rapidly. *I must be dreaming. I ate that Chinese food and passed out at my desk.*

"I wish that was true," I tell him, stepping closer. "I assume you've drawn blood before?" He nods. "More than twice?" I shoot a quick glance at Peter. Noah frowns, but nods again. *A hundred times—* "Good. Then right now, I need you to take some samples."

"Samples?"

"Yes," Peter interjects. "So we can begin tests and observations."

I'm going to puke. Noah thinks.

"I prefer you puke before you stab me with a needle and not during so..." I gesture to the door. "If you need a moment..."

Noah hesitates, loosening the tie at his throat. "No. I-I—" He takes a deep inhale. "Oh, god. Peter," he turns on his heels, facing Peter. "You are in deep shit, man."

Peter gives an awkward chuckle. "Yeah, and now you're here with me, stepping all over it."

After a few minutes talking about the compound with Peter, using terminology I'm not familiar with and tune out immediately, Noah finally slips on a pair of gloves and rolls his stool to me. As I watch his movements, I notice his hands are shaking. *How is she so calm?* His mind flickers with concern. *I'm freaking out!*

I glance at Peter, focusing on his thoughts. *I hope he doesn't tell anyone... not yet.*

Schooling my features because I don't want them to know I'm listening, I focus my attention on the dents in the table. I try to tune out their panic, but I'm feeling overwhelmed too, and all three of us cannot freak out at the same time. By Noah's sweating brow and Peter's sudden pacing, the boys are winning that battle. I take a breath and remind myself to stay calm.

I suck in my bottom lip, not wanting to admit any of my current fears. What if the tests show something dangerous? Something eating away at my insides? What if I die? *Oh, god! What if this shit kills me?* I feel the sting of the needle pierce my skin. *My family... What will they do without me?* The inevitable motherless children wasn't something I ever wanted to think about. I've never *had* a reason to worry about it! But suddenly, my mind is awash with Cheyanne and Max, tears streaking their dirty faces while the ASPCA music sounds in the background. I pale at the thought. *No, they'll always have Peter.* I try to calm myself.

Taking in a deep breath, Noah swaps the filled tube with an empty one. *Don't pass out. Don't pass out.* His thoughts interrupt my panic, and I notice him watching me with wide-eyes.

"I'm not going to pass out," I promise. "And I hope you aren't either." I tilt my head, examining his pale hue.

Noah puffs his cheeks as he exhales. "Sorry. No, I'm not going to pass out. You just look a little pale." He withdraws the needle, replacing it with a cotton ball.

"So do you," I remark, taking over the pressure of the cotton as Noah turns to clean up the supplies.

"You okay?" Peter asks softly, replacing the space where Noah just stood. I nod, and suddenly everything hits me. Voices stream through my mind endlessly making it hard to think clearly and I close my eyes for a moment to try and clear them. I turn, setting my elbows in the indents on the table and drop my head into my hands.

"What if the tests come back... poorly?" I whisper. Peter slips into the seat beside me and he rubs small circles on my back. "This could all be very, very bad."

"Jane." He says my name as though it was his life support; breathing through it and holding onto the moment as long as possible. "I'm not going to let anything happen to you. Do you understand?" He draws me to him in an awkward seated hug. Resting my chin on his shoulder, I breathe in his familiar scent. *This is all my fault, but I can fix this. Trust me,* he tells me silently.

Releasing our embrace, my gaze flickers to our new teammate. "And Noah?" Peter's brow quirks in confusion. "He's kind of freaking out," I say with a slight chuckle.

"Not kind of," Noah chides, packing the blood samples into a travel container. "A hundred percent."

We all share an awkward laugh, watching each other.

Peter checks his watch and stands. "Our next lab begins soon. We should probably—"

"I'll take these and run some preliminary tests," Noah says. "My last course doesn't begin until four." He tucks the case under his arm and heads toward the door.

"Thank you," Peter replies. "And Noah," his tone is edged with desperation as Noah pauses, glancing over his shoulder. "Please keep this between us. For now."

Noah nods then looks at me. *For now.* His thoughts whisper into my mind.

When the door closes, I stand, wiping my sweaty palms on my jeans. "So, what am I supposed to do now?"

"Try not to break anything?" A small smile tugs at Peter's lips.

"Ha. Ha." With a roll of my eyes, I step toward the exit. "Seems like a waste to not do *something* with these abilities." I reach for the handle, ready to be in the warmth outside and away from the sterile lab. Peter follows me, but pauses at the doorway. I turn in the hall to face him. "You think there's any good that will come of this?"

Peter lifts one shoulder, leaning against the doorframe. "I certainly believe so, but if anything starts to feel off—double vision, hallucinations, vomiting, etc.—tell me right away. And if you feel any pain go straight to the hospital."

Pursing my lips, I nod. Adverse side-effects... I've not had anything *bad* going on inside me. The opposite actually. "I will. See you at dinner." I give Peter a quick smile then walk away.

The warm air hits my face as I exit the science building and I breathe it in deeply. Thoughts spin through my mind, but I don't pay attention to them. My head is jumbled with ideas. Ways to use what's been given to me in a time when I feel so, so unimportant and defeated. Perhaps I was meant to drink that not-Gatorade and become whatever this new and improved Jane I am now.

Listening listlessly to the chatter of thoughts around me, I head to the van. Ideas spiral through my mind, but one sticks out above the others. When someone gets special powers... What do they normally do? I believe I know the answer.

CHAPTER 8

After leaving the university, I swing by Starbucks and grab drinks for me and the kids. I think we all deserve a treat after our day. When I arrive at Max's school, there's a few minutes until the end of day bell rings, so I open my phone to browse Amazon. I add a few items to my cart that claim "same-day" delivery, then hit submit. With what I've purchased, and some items from the garage, I think I can pull something together that makes sense. It will surely be *the* surprise of the year for my family!

With a smirk, I sip my mocha with extra whip, feeling proud. Being super may just be exactly what I've needed. The fact that I've been spinning career ideas through my mind with nothing sparking joy concerned me, but now I have these powers and there's something *special* about me. My plan isn't exactly the social work I imagined, but it is a start. A start of something fantastic, I believe. Using these powers, perhaps I can do something good for this community outside of keeping the bedroom magic alive.

The van door flies open and Max jumps in. "Hey, Supermom!"

"Hey, Superson! How was school?" I hand him a hot chocolate after he's buckled. He grins from ear to ear.

"Hot chocolate? Thanks!" He sips it noisily as he settles. "School was great. I need to pick a topic for our upcoming essay assignment."

I shake my head. "An essay in fourth grade? That's insane." Sometimes I think the school system is pushing our kids too hard. Not that Max isn't capable, but not every child is as excelled in writing. "You're so creative," I say, backing out of my parking space. "I'm sure you'll think of an awesome topic."

Cheyanne's school is only a few blocks away. When we pull into the roundabout for pick up, Max spots her instantly.

"Ew, gross!" He gags. "She's talking to that boy with the hair."

I kiss my teeth in annoyance, noticing a teenager boy with wild dark hair bleached at the end. It reminds me of some weird anime character. I wail on the horn. Cheyanne glares, but says her goodbyes and slides into the passenger seat. Jamming her backpack onto the floor, she jerks her seatbelt on.

"Embarrassing much," Cheyanne scoffs, crossing her arms over her chest, then stares out the window.

I nudge her shoulder with the caramel frappe I got her. "It's my job to embarrass you. Have some caffeine to cheer you up."

Cheyanne glances at the peace offering, then snatches it with a grimace. After an initial sip, she pops her EarPods in and resumes ignoring us.

Tapping the steering wheel happily, I hum along to the radio. A Taylor Swift song I'm not familiar with, about needing to calm down, pops on, but I'm not calming down because I'm fired up. Electric shocks run through my veins. My body is a ball of energy waiting to be expelled. Plus, this beat is uplifting and I can't help but bob my head.

I'm buzzing with adrenaline because I've decided. This mom is going to embrace her super-ness and kick some ass. Screw pleasure parties, I'm about to turn everything around with this mistake I've made. All I need to do now is get my family on board with this insane idea!

Two packages are on the front porch when we pull into the driveway. *Nice work, Amazon!*

Cheyanne withdraws her headphones. "I didn't order anything," she confesses, as if afraid I'm about to throw the blame on her. *T. Swift is right, you need to calm down, girl.*

"I know," I tell her with a smile. "They're mine."

Max races to the front porch to examine them.

Cheyanne's eyebrows raise in surprise. "What did *you* order? More cleaning supplies?" She leans over Max's shoulder to read the label, but I take the boxes and duck under the garage door.

"You'll see," I sing, slipping into the house.

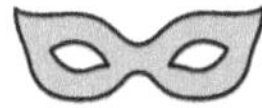

While the kids are in their rooms working on homework, I unpack all the Amazon boxes and spread out my purchases on the bed. I run my fingers over the fabric. It's soft, simple, and thankfully appears to be true to size.

Music drifts through the Bluetooth speaker on my nightstand, something funky and fast that sets my adrenaline racing and helps drown out any thoughts from the kids. I shimmy into the outfit, stretching it over my wide hips. When it feels secure, I move before the mirror to study my reflection. My eyebrows raise at what I see.

The suit is daring and fitting. *Very* fitting. Probably the tightest thing I've worn since the one year I was on the dance team in high school. Those leotards hid *nothing*, but this has smoothed out my figure making my curves appear dramatic and fierce. The shiny leather is practically my second skin, but with the high waist, they look flattering to my curvy figure.

"Oh, Jane," I coo at my reflection, turning to check out the back. "What will your family think of you now?"

As gracefully as I can, I remove the outfit and lay it on the ironing board. There's one more addition I need to make to finalize this statement, and then, to reveal my plan to Peter and the kids.

After dinner, I instruct my family to wait for me in the living room because I have an announcement to make. Peter grumbles about needing to grade papers and Cheyanne rolls her eyes, but complies. The only one excited about my secret project is Max, and his thoughts are exactly on track with what's about to happen.

With bare feet, I skip down the stairs and peek around the doorframe to the living room. Cheyanne's thoughts hit my mind first, filling my head with complaints and annoyance. Then Peter who is trilling over his lab schedule for tomorrow, and finally Max, who is deep into a Spiderman comic.

"Close your eyes," I order from my hiding place. "And no peeking!" I count to three and steady my racing heart. "Are they closed?"

"Yes," everyone answers.

Taking one last breath of bravery, I step into the living room and place myself in front of the couch. Cheyanne has her manicured hand over her eyes, her head flung back dramatically as if she'd just swooned. Max is sitting on the edge of his cushion, fingers tapping his forehead with anticipation. He always loves a good surprise. Peter sits comfortably, but I see his jaw ticking as he waits with eyes closed.

"Don't open them yet, but," I begin, "When I tell you to, don't comment. Okay? Let me explain before you... well... just let me say my bit first."

Ugh. Seriously. This is so lame. Cheyanne grumbles. *I need to make a hair appointment. Why do I keep forgetting?*

I wonder if it's a puppy! I hope it's a puppy. Max exclaims.

I hate surprises... hate them. Peter groans. *Did I bring home those essays?*

I sigh internally, partly annoyed. I want their undivided attention. Something I rarely, if ever, ask for. I can sense their growing impatience and Cheyanne sighs loudly. As if giving their own mother a moment of their time is asking too much.

Shifting my feet shoulder width apart, I slip the lacy mask over my eyes. I ball my fist and place them on my hips. *You got this,* I tell myself.

"Okay. Open your eyes."

Max throws his hands from his face first. His already wide-eyes sparkle and his jaw drops. Cheyanne removes her hand, mid eye-roll, only to spring forward on the couch and gape at me. Peter, however, removes his hand, trails his eyes from my head to my toes, then shakes his head as if ensuring he is awake.

"Honey, wh—"

"Hush! Let me speak first."

What the fuck is going on? This has to be a joke.

I point a finger at Cheyanne. "Watch your language."

"Mom, what the hell are you wearing?" Cheyanne stands, her hands gesturing at me furiously. "Is that? Mom..." She pauses, cocking her head in shock. "Are you wearing *lingerie* around the house?" *Oh, my God! I'm going to die. Right here. Dead.* Cheyanne covers her eyes, flopping back onto the couch.

"No, it's a *supersuit!*" Max chimes, coming to my rescue. "It's awesome!"

Peter clears his throat. "Um, Jane. Honey? Why don't you explain what this is about?"

"I'm *trying,*" I groan. Removing my lace mask, I clutch it between my sweaty palms. My cheeks burn with anger and embarrassment at their reactions. Sure, I'm standing before them in form fitting pleather, silk gloves, and a sleep mask I cut holes into, I'm not wearing a bikini and screaming that I'm joining *Baywatch*!

I'll admit I feel fierce in this get-up, and I'm not going to let their confusion or concerned faces bring me down. I'm going to just own this superhero thing because I *believe* I'm killing it in this teal color.

"I want to help people," I begin, fingering the yellow mask in my hand. "These powers I have... maybe I was destined to get them. I-I can use them to do something *good* and worthy of my time." My cheeks puff as I let a breath out between my pursed lips.

Glancing between my family members, they're frozen in place. Even their thoughts are silent, waiting for whatever I'm about to say next.

Licking my lips, I continue, "I can hear what people are thinking, and I'm getting better at focusing on single thoughts or people at a time, or even tuning someone out completely. It could be useful in all kinds of situations."

"Situations?" Peter's brows furrow.

Cheyanne folds her hands in her lap. "Like what, mom?"

Max looks to either side of him, eyeing his dad and sister as if the answer is obvious. "Are you serious? Bank robbery. Hostage situation. Terrorist attacks," he lists, ticking them off his fingers. "If mom can hear what the villains are thinking, she will know their moves before they do them. Mom would have the bigger hand," he states matter-of-factly.

"The *upper hand,* chimp." Cheyenne glares.

I wrinkle my nose at Cheyanne. "Max is right. And I don't need a lot of sleep. I have this weird supercharge thing, so I can stay out late and still be here to take care of you all."

Confidence is warming within me, and I stand a little straighter.

I believe in my truth more now that it's out there. "Also, this super strength—"

"Wait, what?" Cheyanne blurts.

Max pumps his fists into the air. "Mom is so cool!"

"I accidentally put a dent in a table at your dad's lab today."

No way! So cool! Max thinks.

Holy shit, Cheyanne groans.

I stare at Peter. He hasn't said a word, but he rubs the back of his neck before steepling his fingers to his nose. "Jane. This is a lot to digest."

"Well, obviously." I chuckle because, of course, it's a lot! I'm feeling *a lot* and there is a lot happening inside me I don't fully understand yet. But this is what I want.

"There are a lot of factors working here. Things we haven't even thought about considering yet. And we are still waiting for the test results to come back."

"I'm not running out tonight to fight crime, Peter. I just want to keep everyone on the same page with what I'm thinking."

Peter exhales sharply. "I don't think you're *thinking* through this at all!"

"Well, I know there's things to work out—"

"How are you going to find crime? How will you know if you can help? You aren't trained to fight, Jane." He rubs his hands down his face. "Have you thought about what would happen if whatever situation you're running into, the people have guns? A knife? Heaven forbid, a fucking bomb!" Peter's voice rises in frantic panic and he slumps against the couch. "God, Jane. Be real."

He wants me to look at the bigger picture, and that's fair because honestly, I haven't. My mind went from fear of having no income, to the shock of a lifetime with these powers, and now I want to do what... be a superhero? His words make me backpedal. Perhaps I'm being delusional.

"I think this is amazing," Max says, his voice soothing. I shoot him a grateful smile.

"Guns... knives... mom," Cheyanne begins, shaking her head. "Can't you just, I don't know, stay off in the distance and be an anonymous caller or helper or whatever. You seriously think you can just jump in and be a superhero?" She scoffs. "They're not *real*, mom."

"Yes, they are!" Max argues.

Cheyanne fumes, glaring at Max. "Then you're as insane as she is!"

"Enough. Okay. I hear you. I hear *all* of your concerns. I'm not going to race into the night and pretend like I can take on armed robbers or... or stop a bomb from exploding. I'm not suicidal."

Just deranged. Cheyanne thinks.

Maybe the compound is altering her brain chemistry. Peter muses.

Balling my fists into my hips, I huff in frustration. "Listen. I'm not *deranged* or *insane* or whatever it is you think is wrong with me, Peter." I glare at him and he blanches, knowing I heard what he was thinking. "Why can't I want to do something with my life that has meaning?" I drop my hands to my sides. "Why can't I want something exciting and... and fantastical to happen to *me*?"

"Isn't being our mom enough?" Cheyanne wonders in a concerned tone I rarely hear from her.

I stare at my daughter, whose eyes are watching, waiting for my reaction. She seems offended that I don't answer right away, but I'm calculating my words carefully. Everyone is on edge right now, more than I had expected.

Releasing my clenched fists, I shake my head. "That's not what I meant. I love you all. Being your mom *is* who I am. Who I have been since the day you were born, Cheyanne. I want to be *more* than that because you won't need me to guide you forever." I smile at her. "You're already so independent. You two barely need me."

"That's not true," she objects.

"People look at me and see a chunky mom. Someone who they envision sitting on the couch watching Hallmark movies and eating ice-cream all day between loads of laundry. They form opinions about me based on my appearance and what they think of my life. The moment I tell them my job is to raise my kids and create a welcoming home is the moment they stop seeing me as more than just a mom. I *am* a mom. Your mom," I say, looking at Cheyanne and then Max. "And that will never change. But they also avoid me because I'm the woman who hosts pleasure parties. I know all their secret fantasies and what they do behind closed doors."

"What does that mean—"

"Hush," Cheyanne scolds, then softens, rolling her eyes. "Just trust me. Don't ask."

I smile. "I want to be more than that. I *am* more than that! I can do more than drive a minivan, or pick up groceries, or sell them dildos and lingerie." I pause, feeling my heart thrum rapidly beneath my chest. "I don't want to be the embarrassment I know you believe I am."

Max's thoughts turn curious. *Dildos...?*

"Mom," Cheyanne begins, leaning forward.

Before she speaks, I raise my hand to finish. "I want to be someone you're proud of, Cheyanne. A mom worthy of your praise and adoration."

My eyes drift over each family member. Max is nodding in agreement, eager for whatever is next. He is supportive and determined. Peter's face is clammy and pale. His mouth opens like a fish, but no words come out. Cheyanne, with her flushed cheeks, pushes to the edge of the couch.

"You know we don't think you're an embarrassment, mom," Cheyanne says. "*I* don't think you're an embarrassment," she adds, whisper soft. "I mean, what you do to make money is kind of sketchy. Selling sex toys to my friends' parents... what kid wouldn't be ashamed of that? But you're my *mom*. You're supposed to be boring and watch TV in your pajamas all day. Aren't you? You gave us life, raised us, you take care of the house. You deserve that time, don't you?"

I flinch, as if her words have physically pierced me. Emotions spiral through me like rapid gunfire. I'm proud of her for speaking her mind, but also hurt that she doesn't want more from me.

"I don't want to be boring."

"Mom." Cheyanne sighs, and I can hear in her tone she's about to argue with me.

"No," I stop her. "What kind of role model would I be to you all and to new moms out there if I'm just a boring mom who gets fat and folds laundry? What kind of life is that? It doesn't show you how strong and important people like me are. It doesn't show anyone that even if you want kids, it doesn't mean you can't have a life of your own and be something. It doesn't teach Max to expect more from his future spouse to be supportive of whatever they want to do. It won't teach you, Cheyanne, to reach for the stars and be whatever you want to be, and to stand up for yourself if someone tries to drag you down and put you in a box, labeling you as *one* thing." My voice cracks, and I take a breath to calm myself. "It won't teach either of you to believe in yourselves, because so far, I haven't believed in *myself*."

I press a hand against my chest, sinking into the open chair. "You two have been, and will always be, my world. But what society doesn't always see or give credit to is the instrument that shaped those worlds; your mom. Me." I flatten my palm against my chest. "Mom's have expectations, just like you do, trying to fit into society. I've raised you both to be strong willed and smart. I've pushed you to be brave in any situation, but I want to show you how to wield your own true selves. I want to inspire you because moms are a frickin' force!" I grin through teary eyes. "And I think it's time to change the stigma. It's time for us moms to kick some ass of our own and prove to everyone that we *are* capable of more than doing dishes and running fundraisers. We can achieve something amazing! We can live our own true lives, too, and still be the pajama mom on the block."

Peter, Cheyanne, and Max exchange looks of confusion with each other. Looks that slowly turn to understanding as I observe them.

"Okay," Cheynna agrees. *I can't believe we're doing this,* she thinks, crossing her arms over her chest.

Max's mind is thrumming with an upbeat melody. He's developing an epic theme song for me, unable to stop grinning, while Peter sits stoic. His hands are clasped together under his chin as he leans his elbows on his knees.

My wife is a superhero, he thinks.

"Super*mom.*"

No one speaks, but their eyes all shift to me. After a moment of awkward silence, Cheyanne claps her hands together and stands. "Okay, if you're really going to do this, we need to talk about this outfit because I'm not letting you go outside looking like this."

"Like what?" I wonder, glancing at my outfit.

"Where did you get those pants? I'm pretty sure this form of pleather is illegal."

I shrug. "Amazon."

"And the lettering. P.S.? What does that even stand for, Plus Size?" Cheyanne raises a single brow.

With a scoff, I stand, staring her down. "Rude. Although, I guess it fits, too."

Max covers his mouth to hide a giggle.

"No, Cheyanne. P.S., like the end of a letter. A PostScript. An afterthought," I keep adding explanations because she hasn't written a letter to anyone since she was in elementary school, let alone added a PostScript to anything. "Just your average, plus-size mom trying to save the world. As in, we aren't really the type you think of first when trouble strikes, we are an—"

"Afterthought," Cheyanne finishes with a smile. "I get it."

Peter tilts his head, then nods once. "That's quite a stretch." He chuckles. "But I actually like it. It's quite fitting and makes a statement."

"But it's your name," Max points out.

"Jane is a pretty average name," I argue. "And I said I didn't want to hide who I am. I shouldn't need a secret identity."

"P.S. Jane. It's good," Peter assures, standing and wiping what I assume are sweaty palms on his jeans. "And this is really what you want to do?"

I nod eagerly. "It is. And if it becomes too dangerous, or aliens start invading like they did in that movie..." I snap my fingers, trying to think of the name.

"Like in Marvel movies," Max suggests.

"Yes. Like in those. Thank you, Max." I shoot him a wink. "If something like *that* happens, then we rethink our stance. I'm not running out tonight to fight crime, but I want to put this out there for us to get used to the idea. I *do* want to help this community, and this is how I can do that."

I better get a car out of this, Cheyanne thinks, but she *is* nodding her head in agreement with my statement.

I face Peter, trying to listen to his thoughts, but he's guarded, unable to decide if he is in or out for sure.

"Peter? What are you thinking?" I wring my hands nervously.

As Peter takes a long inhale, I wait. "I think..." He lets out a measured exhale. "I think we need to set up some sort of command center here."

I cock my head in thought. "Yes, that's a good idea."

"If something happens while you're out there, you'll need to contact us. Fast. Especially if things go pear-shaped or you get hurt." He removes his glasses, rubbing his tired eyes. "We have a lot to plan and discuss. You need some sort of basic training."

"Like kickboxing," Max chimes, jumping to his feet and throwing punches and kicks at an invisible foe.

I chuckle. "Yes. That would be a great idea. My mind reading skills aren't going to defend me if someone is trying to slap me in the face... other than knowing it's coming a second before it happens... I guess." I purse my lips in thought. There really *is* a lot to consider still.

"And your *job* job?" Cheyanne wanders, folding her arms over her chest.

"I don't have any parties in my books and I won't be scheduling any more. Most of my merchandise is gone thankfully. Not having parties to worry about will give me plenty of time to hone in on some skills," I say. "And then..." I shrug.

Max jumps onto the couch, fists at his hips in his best superhero pose. "And then you kick some ass, Supermom."

Peter stands, taking my hands in his. "We are here for you. Whatever you need. Our family is your team, Jane. If you think this is what you're supposed to do, then I say yes. Let's do this. But we do this together."

CHAPTER 9

F our other women stand in a circle chatting as I enter the gym. As I set my purse down, I feel their eyes on me. Taking a deep breath, I plaster on a smile, and walk toward them.

"Hello," I say with a wave.

All three reply with a "hi" or "hello", opening their circle a bit to allow me in. One thing I notice right away is that I'm the oldest in the group. Signing up for a self-defense course at the university was the easiest, and cheapest, way to get started with my training, but that also meant being in a room with college-age students.

A door clips shut, and tennis shoes squeak toward us. I shift my weight and turn, wanting to see who the newcomer is, and see a woman I recognize from a recent party.

"Hello, everyone. Welcome to—Oh, Jane," she blanches noticing me. "I-I didn't know you were joining this class."

I shrug. "Teresa, hi. Yes, I uh, I signed up at the last minute. Peter said there were a few openings left."

"Right." She nods, chewing on her inner cheeks. With a forced smile, Teresa glances at everyone else waiting for an introduction. Tugging on her zip up, she clears her throat. "Well, that's great. Nice to see a familiar face. Everyone, I'm Teresa Miller. I not only teach self-defense courses in the evening, but during the day I also train the girls' track and field team." Unzipping her jacket, she tosses it on the bench beside my purse then faces us, rubbing her hands together mischievously. "Let's begin with quick introductions. Since we are all going to be in close quarters the next few weeks, it would be best to at least know who we are working with."

We all share a chuckle.

"Tell us your name, year, and why you're attending this course."

A girl with a long blonde ponytail raises her hand and begins speaking. "I'm Gracie. Junior. And I'm here to just try something new."

"Great. Thank you, Gracie," Teresa says then glances at the next woman.

"Hi. I'm Jamie. Freshman. My mom wanted me to take the course for safety." She shrugs, wrapping her thin arms around herself.

Teresa chuckles. "Nothing wrong with that. One can never be too safe."

"I'm Cora. Junior. I'm taking this because the kickboxing course was full," a girl with dark, tight curls remarks.

Teresa nods, moving on to the next participant.

"Hey, My name is Nichole. I'm a Senior, and I'm here because I listen to a lot of true crime podcasts, so... that's why I'm here."

Teresa snorts and we all laugh. "Fair enough."

And then it's my turn. I gulp and clasp my hands before me. "Hi, I'm Jane. I don't actually attend the university as a student, but my husband is a professor here."

"Who?" Cora interrupts.

"Peter McKenna."

"Oh, I took his course last year. He's tough," Nichole replies, then nudges me. "You should tell him to lighten up some."

I smile. "I'll get right on that."

"Okay, now that we know each other, let's begin with the basics."

Teresa explains what we can look out for. Being aware of our surroundings and recognizing certain situations is the best way to avoid being trapped in an unwanted position in the first place. For me, this came easily as I could hear each member's thoughts as they approached me in their own predatorial way. Teresa applauded my "natural ability" to be in tune with my environment and praised me when I was the only one who could successfully sneak up on her without her being aware of my motives. She made it too easy going down a checklist in her mind of everything around her. As soon as she noticed me, I'd pretend to be on my phone, tying my shoe, or something that wasn't as suspicious as she initially intended.

Once we all got used to being aware, Teresa showed us how to position ourselves if someone grabbed from behind. Locking an arm around our throat, she tugged, explaining how to not only remain calm and aware still, but how to maneuver our hands so when shifting, could break free of the hold.

Two hours later, my body ached in places I didn't think were possible. Teresa worked through three different scenarios, going step by step through body positions, negotiation techniques, and simple ways to evade and escape.

With a groan, I fall onto the couch, letting the soft cushions absorb me. Peter chuckles from the doorway then slinks into the room.

"Tough night?" he asks, sitting beside me.

I tuck my head onto his shoulder. "I would have never guessed how strong Teresa was." Peter laughs. "But you were right, she's a great teacher. I already feel pretty confident with what we learned tonight."

"Confident enough to take on the bad guys?"

I snort. "Depending on how quick they move," I tease. "I'm no professional yet, but if anyone comes at me with the three moves we learned tonight, I'll be ready." With a sigh, I curl my legs up and snuggle closer. "Or I'll be flat on my ass."

Peter snickers. "Oh, you got a package today." I glance up at him and he nods to the small table by the front door. A brown box sits with the iconic Amazon tape. I jump up and snatch it then resume my place on the couch. "What did you order?"

Tearing into the box, I toss the large air bubble packaging onto the floor, and withdraw a smaller box. "Clearly a box for my box." We share a chuckle and then I flash him the white carton. "It's a police scanner."

His eyebrows raise. "Seriously?"

"Yup." I struggle with the tape until finally, I give up and rip the top off. A small device tumbles out with the instruction manual.

"Is this even legal?" Peter straightens, inching close to examine the item.

"It is. I looked it up before ordering it." I page through the instructions, looking for the quick set-up guide. "The last thing I need is to be arrested for listening in on local police business."

"Right," he says, drawing the word out. "But what happens if you get caught?"

"Caught doing what?"

Peter scoffs. "Saving the day, Supermom." His tone is edged with mockery.

I set the police scanner in my lap and face him. With furrowed brows I stare at him, uncertain what he means.

"Look," he begins, shifting on the couch and looking at me like he's about to explain something to a five year old. I raise a single brow and he clears his throat and the smug look on his face. "When you show up to apprehend someone, or drop into some insane situation, what do you think the cops will do when they find you?"

"Say thank you?"

Peter rolls his eyes. "I doubt they'll be grateful when you're stomping all over a crime scene or getting in their way. What happens if you cause more damage than whatever the bad guy is doing? Do you think they'll let you off with just a warning? 'Oh, no big deal P.S. Jane. Town insurance will cover the extra thousands of dollars you just cost us. Next time try not to make such a big mess.'" When I don't answer right away, he leans forward slightly. "Well?"

"I would imagine they wouldn't be too happy... I suppose." Honestly, the idea of getting in their way never crossed my mind. Why wouldn't they be grateful for my help?

Peter sighs, shaking his head. "I wish you wouldn't jump into this so quickly. This isn't something you can just dive into."

"Would you rather I stand around, dipping my toes in, hoping the minnows won't nibble at my feet?"

"Yes! Because the other option is taking a deadly leap of faith and fending off the sharks!" His voice raises. "Jesus, Jane."

Tears well in my eyes. Rarely does Peter get enraged about anything. "I thought you supported me."

"I do," he says, running his fingers through his hair. "But this isn't like the movies or-or the comics that Max reads." Peter slumps into the couch, tossing his hands into the air. "This is real life, Jane. Real people. Real situations. Real *danger*. I assumed by agreeing to all of this we would take it slow, not run off into the night merely days later." Closing his eyes, he takes two deep breaths. "You're not ready."

I gulp. Perhaps he's right. I never considered any legality of what I'm doing. In the movies, they just show up and get shit done and rarely do people complain... except in *The Incredibles 2*, that was a hot mess! But me? If the cops found P.S. Jane kicking ass at a scene, what *would* they do?

Tapping my finger on my thigh, I consider Peter's concerns. They're legitimate, I'll give him that, but I can't wait around to be 100 percent ready because that will never happen. Some things I need to learn as I go.

"I'll look into the police involvement stuff," I replied, fluttering my hand. "But that doesn't mean I can't test out the equipment."

"Jane..."

"Taking the police scanner out for a spin won't get me in trouble. It's totally legal, remember?" I face him, feeling the excitement bubble up inside me. "I-I can take it and listen in and see how far the range is. Just listen and take notes. I need to study up on the police codes anyway, so this will only be practice until we all feel more comfortable with the legal and bad-assery side of this super thing."

Peter sighs through his nose. "Fine."

I beam, grabbing the instructions again.

"But promise me you will not, under any circumstances, go out and try to save the day?"

"Fine," I tell him, crossing my toes. "I won't jump into anything crazy."

"You here for some convention or something, lady?"

I take a foil wrapped hotdog from the vendor and a Pepsi, then glance down at my handmade supersuit. My cheeks burn.

Must be a full moon, the older man wonders, eyeing me cautiously.

I half forgot I was even wearing it. Cheyanne helped update a few of the "intimate items," and I wanted to wear the outfit as much as possible to get used to the fit. The suit is tight, like *really* tight, and having all of myself out there would take some getting used to. There is no hiding stomach rolls in this thing, and the more I wear it, the more comfortable I will feel.

I promised Peter I would stay in the car—recon only; we agreed—but listening to the scanner made me twitchy, and my legs ache from sitting so long. I tried switching to the radio, but then I forgot I was supposed to be paying attention to the scanner, and then I was hungry... like *starving*... and I couldn't ignore my grumbling stomach anymore. Even though we live in a small town, it's a university town, and we have late-night snackeries for those out at the bars, events, or students up late studying. This little hot dog stand is my savior, and thankfully, close to the parking lot where I've set up to listen to the scanner.

"A convention?" I ask, squirting ketchup on my hotdog.

The vendor raises a thick gray brow. "Like a comic thing. You dressin' up like one of those supers from the movies?" *Who is she supposed to be? Wonder Woman? Bat Girl? No... she's something else,* he considered internally as his eyes drifted over my figure.

I take a bite of the hot dog and nod. "Kind of."

A couple jingling their keys nears. When they notice me, they slow and their eyes grow wide. The man grips the woman's elbow, leading her away. *Jesus, I knew we should have parked at the other lot.* His thoughts trail as he hurries down the sidewalk.

"Be safe out there," the hot dog man calls out, squinting at my chest. "P.S. Jane." With a wink, he resumes checking the rotating hotdogs. *Them crazies be out tonight.*

A grin overtakes me as I head back to the car, thinking about the poor couple that noticed a plump woman in a skintight suit stuffing her face with cheap hotdogs. I giggle because I'm sure I appear to be a bit on the insane side.

I notice a man crossing the street toward the vendor, his eyes on me. *What in the hell...* he croaks, but I roll my eyes and continue, disappearing around the corner.

It becomes a game for me; tuning into bystander's thoughts as they pass my car. I start a list on the back of a receipt, checking boxes in different categories of what they're thinking about: food, exams, drinks, sex, and other. It helps to pass the time and before I know it, the clock reads 3 a.m. The scanner still sits silently.

With a defeated huff, I turn the key in the ignition and decide to go home. Nothing was happening tonight. Even though I wasn't planning on intervening, I was secretly hoping for something big to go down. Listening in on that would have been like reality TV—addicting and heart-pounding. At least I know the scanner works, and I had time to read the entire instruction manual front to back. Three times. I know what every knob and button does, and I wrote some codes I overheard while officers passed along information. I want to know ones to pay attention to for something juicy, like a robbery or a fire or... I'm not sure. Something. But tonight is not that night.

With a heavy sigh, I turn the key. Pulling out of the parking lot, I make my way home to my waiting pajamas and cozy bed.

CHAPTER 10

I'm the first parent to arrive at the PTA meeting, and I take my usual seat at the end of the table. Setting down a Starbucks for myself and one for Lynn, I withdraw my notebook from my bag. This morning, after I finished some chores, I sat and wrote a list of ideas for today's meeting. I glance through them as I wait for everyone else to arrive, eager to share my thoughts. Already, two pages are filled with concepts for community service, school recycling, and I even added a few things about the upcoming holiday season. Go, me!

Footsteps tap behind me. I don't need to look at who it is because I already know.

Hello everyone! Thanks for coming today. This week we are preparing for the school fall clean up and food drive—Rebecca's thoughts pause. *What the hell?* She thinks, and I swivel to face her.

"Jane," Rebecca chitters, sending a shiver down my spine. Her voice hits me like Sweet'N Low, overly sweet and totally fake! Not quite what you want in your mouth... or ears. "You're early. And you brought... doodles?" She flutters her one free hand toward my notebook as she passes.

"Rebecca. Hello." I flash her a smile. "I *am* here and I brought notes for the meeting today."

Rebecca's mauve lips purse, and her eyes narrow. "Well, I'm sure it will thrill us to hear them." She turns, making her long dark hair fling around her in a rush. The movement reminds me of a raven flapping its wings. *Who does she think she is? I'm the PTA president. I have the ideas for the season. Not her.*

"Already ruffling some feathers?" Lynn teases, sliding into the seat beside me.

I slide one of the mocha's toward her. "You know I like to make my presence known."

Lynn gasps, grabbing the drink and inhaling deeply. "You shouldn't have. Actually, yes. Yes, you should have. I deserve this. Thank you." She nudges me with her shoulder, then sips the still steaming beverage. "Ah, perfect."

I roll my eyes with a chuckle, then turn my attention to the head of the table, sensing a red fiery glare on me. Rebecca. When our gazes meet, she averts her stare and plasters on a stage worthy grin, but her mind is reflecting the boiling rage I saw in her eyes.

Rude. So fucking rude. Just come in, sit down, and shut up. It's not that hard! Why is this so hard? Rebecca inhales through her nose, then begins, but quickly adjusts her features to show a calm, collective leader as the rest of the PTA members file in and take their seats.

"Hello everyone! Thanks for coming today." Rebecca waits for everyone to look at her. "We are just months away from the holiday season, and I think we should brainstorm for community outreach, our holiday projects, and how we can best support the local shelter."

Rebecca gives Stacy a nod, signaling her to take her place at the easel where a large pad of paper sits. Uncapping a thick, black marker, Stacy waits patiently as Rebecca continues.

"Every year we have the lower grades create decorations for the shelter and bring in gloves and scarves." She takes a breath, providing Stacy time to scribble on the paper. "The upper levels donate coats, shoes, and hats while we also ask for student volunteers to help pass out food items on Saturdays." A smile overtakes her face, as if she alone has orchestrated these events in the past. Little does she remember, the idea for weekly volunteers actually came from Brandon, three years ago. He's a quiet, robust man, who'd never call her out on it, though.

Rebecca folds her hands before her, glancing at each PTA member. "This has always been an enormous success, and our shelter is so grateful for the extra hands, but," she chirps, tapping a long red nail against the table, "I think this year we can take it up a notch. I'd like to hear some of your ideas about how we can give back even more." Her hawk eyes turn to me. "Jane, why don't you begin? You brought ideas, didn't you?" The edge of her lips curl into a maniacal grin.

"I did," I say, giving her a sweet smile. Thumbing through my notebook, I look for a good idea to begin with. The room is quiet except for the fluttering of pages.

Rebecca's smile grows, showing all her teeth in an unsettling display. *I'll show them what a waste she is on this committee.* "Do you have any ideas? Or are you just bringing doodles in to share?"

That wicked grin doesn't phase me, though, and I flash my own toothy smile back. "Of course. Thanks, *Becca*. I do have some ideas." I clear my throat, finally finding the right page. "While helping in the shelter is perfectly wonderful, we should consider how difficult it can be for these places to get ample food and supplies to ensure everyone has a proper meal, and a safe, warm place to go when the weather turns. Every year, we see families of all sizes and ages come through the line for Thanksgiving and Christmas Eve dinner, but what happens after that? Or before even?" I pause, glancing up. Heads bob in agreement, waiting for my next words. "My concern is that, yes, they go home with full bellies and gently used items, but then do they wonder where their next meal will come from? Can they continue feeding their families for the week?"

A few faces turn into concern as they process my questions.

"What do you suggest, then? We make food every day from November to January?" Rebecca scoffs. "These are *children* volunteers. They need to be in school. We can't simply pull them out every day to work at the shelter."

"No, of course not," I continue, without hesitation. "But we've never considered other options before, either. We could provide these families with more."

"More?" someone asks.

I nod. "What if we provide these families a bag to take home that contains canned goods and boxed items when they come in? Things to help get them through a few days if they needed assistance. Most of us have experienced hard times, I'm sure," I say, shooting Rebecca a subtle glare. I doubt she's felt the pang of struggle at all in her cushy life. "And having pantry items when times get tough can make a difference. Take a little stress off the parents who I'm sure are working double time to make ends meet."

Rebecca rolls her eyes. "Jane," she begins, her voice edged with annoyance.

A PTA dad shushes her. "Let her finish, for God's sake, Rebecca." *We could have used this kind of help last year...* his thoughts whisper into my mind. My heart aches for him and his family. A few other member's remarks brush through as well about past, and current, struggles. All except Rebecca, who has her eyes narrowed at the man. But she keeps her mouth shut.

"I propose we hold a food drive competition for the entire school," I recite proudly.

Rebecca gawks. "A school-wide competition? We've never done such a thing." She waves me off, but the other members are chatting about the idea.

"It will take some planning, something I—"

"And I," Lynn interjects, raising her hand, eager to help.

I give her a thankful smile. "Lynn and I can lead it. We could run the competition right up to the Monday before Thanksgiving break, and the class that has the highest donation count wins a pizza party the day before break," I explain.

"Kids love pizza parties," Stacy chimes, and everyone agrees. Everyone except Rebecca, who is grinding her teeth, glaring at me.

"Every class will have a designated volunteer to count their cans and items, then the teacher will confirm. We can put a big chart in the front office that shows the total number of donations combined. That way, students will see the number growing as a total and it will build the anticipation of the final tally. We will keep a list of each class separately, but it's always fun to see how it all comes together. A big red chart growing and growing."

"And we just take the food to the shelter? That's the plan?" Rebecca snorts.

I shake my head. "Once we collect the items, the center can send a truck to collect it all. We will gather volunteers to help separate food into boxes or bags to hand out. We could start after the Thanksgiving dinner. That way, every family will go home with the donated clothes, full bellies, *and* food for a few days."

"With the entire school involved," Lynn interjects, "we would have enough food collected to supply families for part of the season. We all know how tight budgets can be, especially around the holidays."

"And what about after?" Rebecca remarks, fingers clenching around the edge of the table.

"Well, we can't guarantee to have enough to continue after the holidays, but we could plan a second drive in the spring and try to help restock the local pantry again," I reply.

A PTA mom chimes in eagerly, "Oh, the kids would love an ice-cream party!"

"Yes! Perfect for spring! Thanks, Anna." I shoot her a grateful smile.

A few parents clap, sharing their eagerness about the idea. The members of the PTA continue exchanging ideas, making plans about posters, and begin volunteering their time to help. Rebeccas doesn't seem to move, but I can tell from her still body, she is probably boiling with rage inside. I tune into her thoughts, doing my best to weed out the other chatter.

That bitch, Rebecca thinks. Her lips purse as she notices me watching her.

"I have other ideas, too," I continue, flipping a page in my notebook. "Like an angel tree for local families and some events for the new year. Also, a backpack and school supplies donation for families who are struggling to buy basic classroom needs." I'm smiling so much my cheeks are aching. No one is paying attention to Rebecca. All eyes and thoughts are on me. *Eat that, Rebecca!* I smirk. Everyone is chatting merrily, throwing their own ideas my way. I do my best to write them down, nodding and responding as needed throughout the meeting time.

Lynn nudges me with her shoulder. "You did good, friend!" She leans closer to whisper, "I think Rebecca is about to explode."

If she thinks she's going to take my place... Rebecca's head sways slowly. *She has another thing coming.*

Bring. It. On. I tell her with my thoughts, and I swear her eyes widened ever so slightly, as if she could tell what I was thinking.

It is past 10 p.m. when I get home from another self-defense class. The more time I spend evading fake capture, the more confident I feel. I just hope my confidence shows Peter that he can worry less about my safety.

As I'm filing a glass of water in the dim kitchen, I hear footsteps tap down the steps.

"Hey, Mom," Cheyanne says, sitting at the bar with her iPad. She's in her pajamas. Her hair tied up in a messy bun.

"Hey, sweetie. What are you working on so late?" I sip my water, then lean my elbows on the counter.

Cheyanne chews on her bottom lip and her fingers trace the edges of the tablet. "There's a dance in a few weeks. I thought... I think I'd like to go." She peers at me.

"A dance? That sounds fun. Who are you going with?"

Cheyanne shrugs. "I-I don't know. Just some friends."

"Not a boy?"

Her head sways and I nod, not digging into the topic further. I know she's never committed herself to one boyfriend so far, and my highschool track record of dating wasn't great either. I'm just glad—or at least hoping—she doesn't get treated how I did back then.

When I was a sophomore, a junior named Timmy—a total hottie—asked me to the winter ball. It ended up being a prank. His friends dared him to ask me and then bail at the last second. I spent the night locked in my room, crying my beautiful makeup off, and ripping bobby pins from my updo. It shredded my heart, and I swore to never go to a dance again. And I didn't.

I wouldn't wish that kind of loneliness and sorrow on anyone.

"Going with friends will be way more fun," I tell her, reaching across the table and patting her hand. "Trust me." I roll my eyes, moving back to drink my water. "So, is that what you're looking at, then? Dresses?"

She nods, turning the tablet toward me. "I found a few I really like."

I pick up the device and scroll through the photos. There are pictures of a turquoise gown that reminds me of a Cinderella dress, a dusty rose mermaid style with a flare at the bottom, and a lovely powder blue piece.

I set the iPad down and tap it. "This one."

The blue one is perfect for her complexion. Hanging mid-thigh, it has a lace overlay beginning just above the waistline. It drapes over the hemline, tapering in the back like a small train that will hit just below her knees. It's sleeveless and absolutely lovely, and the sweetheart neckline shows enough skin to make it elegant but modest.

"Yeah?" Cheyanne asks with a grin, drawing the tablet toward her. "I really like this one, too."

"It's stunning. Let's order it."

"I don't know. Do you think it'll be too tight?" *I won't be able to eat a thing!* I hear her concerns.

"With a dress like this, you can easily wear some Spanx underneath and no one will notice it because of this overlay. We can order you some for the dress, too."

Cheyanne beams. "Okay. Yeah. I think you're right." *Spanx will hide everything! But it's $250... she'll never buy it for me.*

I shift from the counter, drawing my wallet from my purse. Taking the bank card, I hand it to her. "Here. Get the dress and then find some Spanx that will fit you."

"Are you sure? It's—"

I lift my hand, shushing her. "I'm sure, Cheyanne. Get the dress. Tomorrow, we will call and make a hair appointment at the salon." When she doesn't move to take the card, I add with a wink, "Dad's treat."

Cheyanne chuckles, taking the card. "Thanks, Mom."

CHAPTER 11

I booked a last minute pleasure party—something I hate to do, but desperate times call for desperate measures. The dildos in the garage are *not* going to sell themselves... and tossing them in the trash seems like such a waste. It's not like I can donate them... gross!

The party ended an hour ago, and I decided to spend a bit of time listening in on the police scanner. It's been quiet so far, but I have an itch in my spine that makes me feel like something is going to happen tonight. I just know it! Until then, I relax and wait.

This is what I'll be doing instead of parties—sitting, waiting for action! It's a weird sensation not having my calendar full of weekend parties. Not having to think about packing sexy items up and lugging them across town. Not having to listen to women bitch and complain about calories or latex allergies. I chuckle to myself, glancing at the bedazzled case in the back. I can finally use the luggage for its intended purpose; traveling!

I could tell Cheyanne was secretly happy that my career as the "sex toy mom" was ending, but her thoughts suggested she wasn't all too thrilled still about having a supermom. She tried to keep her internal comments quiet, and I did my best to stay out of her head, but a few concerns and frustrations found their way to me. Worry about my safety and expecting the worst. She's so much like her father in that way. To help get her involved, and to see it's not going to be as scary as her mind thinks it is, I entrusted her to revamp my supersuit.

And she was thrilled to help!

"We can replace the sex dungeon look now," she told me. I'm pretty sure my jaw hit the floor.

Now, the turquoise skinsuit from *Amazon* accents my curvy shape, and the black pleather bustier, gloves, and skirt add a mysterious element. I sewed a thick yellow thread around the dark material so it matches the stitching in my P.S. Jane lettering. Cheyanne even found a headband with little coffee cups to add a little buzz to the whole ensemble and keep my hair out of my face.

The entire suit comes across as a mix of Mrs. Incredible and Wonder Woman. I have to give Cheyanne credit because I look amazing. I even have pockets! Now, I can walk around in my suit feeling more confident and comfortable in my skin. Not an inkling of dominatrix in my look.

"Everything okay?" Peter's voice crackles through the tiny bluetooth in my ear. We decided it would be best to not walk into a crime scene with a cell phone or walkie-talkie strapped to my belt. This way, Peter can be in contact with me and know if anything goes wrong. But that's a worry for another night, because tonight was just another round of recon and testing myself on police code knowledge.

I chew on the inside of my cheek. "Yes. Just bored. I thought a Saturday night would give us more action. *Any* action. A mugging. Car theft. Jaywalker... something."

"Hm," Peter grunts, and the sound of typing begins.

"What are you working on?" I adjust the dials to the scanner to ensure it's on the proper channel.

The ticking of keys stops. "Looking over some notes from—" Static from the police scanner interrupts him as two officers exchange codes.

Leaning forward, I grip the steering wheel to listen closely.

"Possible 10-62 at 330 Elmont Ave.," a female officer recites.

"Copy. En route," a rough male voice replies.

My adrenaline spikes. "Oh! 10-62... 10-62," I repeat, flipping through the notes on police codes. A 10-62, breaking and entering. "Got one!" I chirp, punching the address into my GPS and starting the van.

"What? Honey, no. Stop! You can't just jump into this." Peter's concern comes through in a loud, hurried tone.

I squeal with excitement. "I just heard a possible breaking and entering. It's close. Like, two minutes away." Already, I'm pulling out of the parking lot, waving to the hot dog man, and gunning it down the road.

"Jane! You're supposed to be *listening* and-and testing equipment," Peter stammers. "You're not ready for this."

With a scoff, I roll my eyes. I know Peter can't see me, but my body is pumping with caffeine, adrenaline, and hot dogs, urging me to go for it.

"Let's consider this a test run. I'll just do a drive-by. Take a look," I say as nonchalantly as I can, even though my heart is pounding so hard I can hear it in my ears.

I turn onto Elmont Ave. and slow to squint at the house numbers. The residences are tall and skinny, making it hard to find the small numbers painted by the doors. But there it is, 330.

"Bingo!" I lock my sights on the brick house and slow to a stop.

Not a single light illuminates the curtained windows, and the porch light remains dark. Either the family is asleep, or the house is vacant. I hope this family is not in the house.

Unbuckling my seatbelt, I roll down my window and peer at the mowed lawn. There's a lonely newspaper sitting on the porch letting me know someone wasn't home to retrieve it this morning.

"Jane?" Peter whispers.

"I'm here." My eyes drift over every window, searching for any sign of movement. "It's quiet. No sign of anyone, inside or out." I glance in the side mirror. "No police yet, either."

A creak sounds on the Bluetooth. I imagine Peter leaning forward in his desk chair in anticipation. In the distance, a dog barks, drawing my attention to the street. Lofty trees loom along the sidewalk, shuddering as a breeze whistles by. Down the road, a street light flickers and a car door slams.

Headlights flood the van, and I press myself against the seat, wanting to make myself as invisible as possible. A small Honda slows, but the driver doesn't glance my way. I exhale, feeling my racing heart ease.

"I'm going to park in the alley," I tell Peter, easing the car from the curb and to the back of the house. There's a chain-link fence closing in the backyard where a wooden swing set sits empty. I stare at the back windows and am about to give up when a light flickers past a kitchen window. It's quick. A single beam. Perhaps a flashlight as someone rushes by.

I haven't tested the distance of my mind reading ability, but what better time than now! Staring at the house, I focus on whoever held the light. Sweat accumulates on the back of my neck. Silence meets me and nothing more.

I ease from the van, closing the door as softly as I can, but the clicking of the latch springs through the bluetooth.

"Jane? What are you doing?"

Damn, he heard. I lower my voice. "I'm getting a closer look. You know, recon."

"Dammit, Jane," his voice booms, making me jump. "Get back in the ca—"

I hit the disconnect button. *Whoops.* His voice is too distracting, and right now, I need to focus on the task at hand.

Taking cautious steps, I keep to the shadows and slink toward the back door. The glass above the knob is broken, and the door is ajar. A light flickers by and I duck to the side, not wanting my figure to cast an outline or shadow anywhere.

Closing my eyes, I fixate on the house and let my mind wander until I find consciousness. A voice billows into my mind as I feel the first thought.

Fuck. Fuck. There's nothing here! A husky tone rings. I let out an exalted sigh of relief that it worked and I can hear what's going on. Another light races by, heading toward the first. I think that means two people are inside.

Xbox. PlayStation. Diamond ring... another voice lists off items.

My pulse thrums, flooding my ears with rapid beats, and my fingers twitch in anticipation. It isn't fear making me on edge; it is excitement! Adrenaline sours through me as I slink through the back door.

Come on! The husky voice groans.

A drawer slams and I freeze. Footsteps pound away from me, heading to the front of the house. I slide into the dark kitchen. I have no idea what I'm doing, but I tiptoe over the glass shards, trying not to make a sound, and head toward the hushed voices arguing.

"Hurry, man!" I recognize the husky tone. Peeking around the corner, a tall lanky figure dressed in dark washed jeans and a black hoodie is bouncing between his feet.

"Shut it! We're almost done," the other replies, ripping cords from the wall to draw the flat screen off its mount. The shorter man is built thicker. I gulp, hoping it isn't all muscle under that thick jacket. Then I do something without even thinking. I step out and click my tongue at them.

Yes. I actually clicked my tongue at them like a disapproving mother. Which I am!

What the fuck? The husky one shouts internally as the other snarls, *Dammit!*

The shorter one shoots to his feet, swinging toward me while withdrawing a knife from the pocket of his slacks. He drops the bag in his other hand, clanking the stolen goods together.

I clench my fists, placing them on my hips, and lift my chin. Digging out my best mom-voice that always sends a shudder through my children, I speak, "I suggest you leave. Now." Sweat drips down the back of my neck in an icy drop. I'm hoping I sound demanding enough as I glance between the two men. They appear unfazed. Confused, really. This is what they do in the movies, right? Stand straight, portray confidence, stay firm... I glance between the two men wondering what I should do next.

After a slight hesitation and a quirk of his brow, the shorter one lunges at me. I side-step him, and using my elbow, ram it into his back as hard as I can. With my extra strength I momentarily forgot about, it is quite a hard hit. He barrels into the carpet, and I wince as the floor lets out a sharp *crack*. Oh, snap! The handful of defense classes I've taken are really coming in handy! Go me!

I shift my gaze to the other, who is frozen.

He lifts his gloved hand in surrender. *Shit. Shit. Shit,* he thinks, hands shaking.

"Look, this wasn't my idea," he trembles.

I step toward him, confidence bubbling because one intruder is not as scary as two. With a smirk, I watch the man's brow furrow. As I near, I cock my head and listen to his thoughts.

"Eh, I wouldn't grab that knife if I were you," I comment, knowing he is considering if he is fast enough to snag the weapon from his belt before I can react.

The intruder's eyes widen, but still the idiot swings his right arm back.

I let instinct take over and swing my knee up like I'm doing some form of fancy marching then press my foot forward with as much force as I can muster. It's not pretty... or completely successful, but the jarring foot-jab sends the man stumbling. I smirk, chuckling under my breath. Now that he's bent and caught off guard, I take my palms and slam them against his shoulders. He flies back, hitting the wall. Picture frames clatter to the ground in shattering pieces.

My self-defense instructor would be so proud!

The man coughs, and his head lolls.

"Who the fuck are you?" a voice from behind me asks. The man I slammed into the carpet is rising on shaking arms. "Some kind of wannabe super?"

I pivot to face the short man struggling to get to his feet. His fingers claw at his chest, trying to catch his breath. I assume the impact knocked the wind out of him. What a shame.

Police lights flash against the front windows. My cue to get the hell out of here.

I take a step toward the short man and he flinches. Pointing to the lettering on my bust, I cock a half smile. "I'm P.S. Jane. And you've committed a crime."

Glass clinks as the taller man rolls to his knees. He coughs, rubbing his back where he collided with the wall.

Keeping them both in my line of sight, I step near the front window and peek out. Two officers are making their way up the walkway, hands at the ready near their guns. I flip the lock so they can enter. The click makes the officers hesitate. They exchange curious glances before proceeding.

I watch them for an instant before Peter's worry floods through me; the conversation about getting caught and things being illegal. I blanch because I never actually took the time to look any of this up yet. And I don't want to find out how much trouble I'll be in if I get caught.

"Time for me to go," I chirp, making a beeline for the back door.

The man is using the dining table as a crutch after I hit him. Reaching into his pocket, I can hear he wants to pull a weapon on me. What kind? I'm not sure because I'm not close enough to see, and in my haste to escape, I've let my concentration slip from their thoughts.

Gingerly, I hop into the van and slip my mask off. I exhale sharply, beaming. My heart is still pounding and I'm lightheaded, as if I'd been holding my breath this entire time.

"Whoo!" I cheer, cranking the radio. I did it! I helped my first victim and totally crushed it.

My fingers trill on the steering wheel like a piano because Shania Twain is on the radio. I belt out "Man! I Feel Like A Woman," the entire way home, not caring that I'm off key because I fucking did it. I *am* a superhero. P.S. Jane.

CHAPTER 12

T he overhead lights of the kitchen click on as I'm tossing my purse onto the counter. I blink at the brightness, swearing.

Peter's arms wrap around me. "Dammit, Jane!" he scolds in my ear, squeezing me. Then, he draws away, eyes flickering over my entire body. "What the hell happened? Are you okay? Why did you turn off the phone?"

Whoops. I was so wrapped up in the moment I forgot to turn the Bluetooth back on.

"Peter," I begin softly. "I'm fine. Stop." I grip his face, staring into his concerned gaze. "Everything went fine." I flash him a reassuring smile.

Peter's face softens, and his shoulders relax under my touch. "Jesus, Jane. What happened?"

My smile widens. "I got the bad guys!"

"What?" he spits.

I release my hands from his face and turn to get a glass of water. I am so thirsty I feel like I could pass out from dehydration.

"There were two guys tossing this house." I recall the events of the evening. Peter sinks into the barstool, listening to every word. In between racing moments, I gulp two glasses of water, then busy myself with prepping the coffee for the morning. Finally, I turn on the dishwasher and conclude my story. "Then the police showed up, so I snuck out the back."

Peter rubs the back of his neck. "And no one saw you?"

I shake my head. "Besides the two robbers, no. I kept my mask on the entire time." I lean my hip against the counter feeling proud of my evening.

"Jane," he sighs, taking off his glasses to rub his eyes. "I cannot believe you'd be so senseless."

"I think you're being a bit harsh," I retort, narrowing my gaze.

Peter's eyes snap to mine. They're full of rage and disappointment. "*Me*? Being harsh?" He spits an unhumorous laugh. "Jane, you could have gotten seriously hurt. They had knives and who knows what other weapons."

"I've been training."

"You've had a handful of lessons. You're not some champion fighter!" His voice is laced with frustration.

I purse my lips to the side to keep myself from saying something I may regret.

I can't fucking believe her. Peter's thoughts whisper into my mind. *She could have been caught.*

"But I wasn't," I say, and when Peter looks at me in confusion I add, "caught. I wasn't caught."

"You aren't thinking clearly. I don't mean caught standing in the middle of a crime scene, you could have left behind any sort of trace evidence—your DNA."

I scoff, but before I can reply, Peter is already speaking.

"Fingerprints. Hair. Any of this ringing a bell?"

"I had my gloves on and my hair was tucked back with the band," I say, pointing to the cute headband. "I'm not going to ever be 100 percent certain a piece of my hair doesn't fall out, or I get so excited I spit, or whatever else you're thinking Peter McKenna!" I seethe. "Even in the movies, nobody's perfect. And you can't expect me to get everything right the first time. How many chances do superheroes get, even when they mess up?"

Peter blinks at me, then shrugs.

"Well, they're still making movies about them, so I guess the count is still going up."

"Even they get caught sometimes, Jane. And you know, this isn't some movie you're playing out. This is real life," he remarks, tapping his finger against the counter for emphasis.

"I know, Peter. I'm not living some neurotic fantasy. Tonight was a rush," I tell him, beaming. "I've never felt that kind of exhilaration in years. It was like... like when the roller coaster plummets and your stomach drops and you can't help but throw your arms into the air and scream with both joy and fear."

Peter exhales heavily and we sit in silence as the clock ticks in the background against the hum of the dishwasher. He doesn't look at me, but I can't help but stare at him. I want some sort of reaction, but his face is unreadable, etched out of stone. I try to not slip into his thoughts again, but they seem to reach out for me in desperation. He's replaying the events of the night I described, his own soothing words an overlay of reassurance that I'm home and safe and fighting won't do us any good.

"We should get some sleep," he blurts.

I blink, watching his serious facade as he stands and moves toward me. My smile falls because I want nothing more than to continue talking about this night. But Peter is done talking. From his thoughts, I can tell this is too much for him. Too sudden. So, I don't push him anymore. Not tonight, at least.

"Oh, yeah. Okay. I-I'll be right up."

Peter kisses my cheek, then disappears up the steps. My heart is finally slowing as the adrenaline wears off in a spiraling, queasy sort of way. The house grows silent again, even so, I stand in the kitchen staring at the staircase. After a moment, exhaustion settles over me and I yawn. Before I head to bed, I want to commemorate the night, and if Peter won't celebrate with me, I have to celebrate alone.

Putting my mask back on, I find my phone in my purse. Snapping some selfies, I save them in a special folder, dubbing it "P.S. Jane's Origin Story." Now, I have something to look back on to remember how badass I felt tonight.

With a victorious grin, I make my way upstairs, slip into my pajamas, and crawl into an empty bed. The water in the bathroom splashes on and I hear Peter sigh through the door. I don't settle under the covers, but wait for him as I lather lotion on my arms and legs. His thoughts easily come to my mind.

How can she be so excited? They could have killed her tonight! Holy hell... what would have happened if they had a gun? They could have shot her and left for dead and I wouldn't have even known because she shut the damn phone off! His words send a wave of guilt over me, draining the last bit of adrenaline. *I couldn't even help her. She was alone and I couldn't... I couldn't save her.*

My chest tightens. I hadn't considered how Peter might have felt when I clicked off the bluetooth, or what he would be thinking sitting in the dark. I was running on such a high I wasn't thinking straight! Peter's right. The idea of the thieves having a gun or bomb or something crazy never crossed my mind. I was in the zone. Consequences out the window!

I slump against the pillows. *I wonder if all supers feel this low when they finish saving the day.*

The bathroom door opens, and Peter shuffles out, climbing into bed. He shoots me a small, but sad, smile then reaches for the light.

"I'm sorry," I say, letting my chin fall to my chest. "I shouldn't have turned off the only communication I had. It was dumb. I just…" I huff, shifting to face him. He's watching me with down-turned eyes. "I couldn't focus on the thoughts of the men with your voice in my ear. You were so loud, shouting at me… and I… I just stopped thinking."

He stares at me. "It's not the first time you've hung up on me." A smile tugs at one side of his lips. "But it is the first time you've run off to be a superhero."

I chuckle. "I know. I'm sorry."

Peter takes my hands and squeezes them. "If we are going to do this, we have to be a team. If something happens to you…" His voice breaks, and he cranes his head away.

"Nothing is going to happen to me. I'll be more careful. More aware. And I promise to not hang up on you again. Not for super things at least," I tease. "It really was stupid of me. You're right."

Peter's eyes widen. "Did you just openly express how *right* I am about something?" He falls back in feigned shock.

"Yes." I giggle. "You. Are. Right," I enunciate each word because he will probably never hear me say it again. "If we are going to work as a team, then I can't just hang up on you for being annoying."

"I was *not* being annoying."

"Peter." I shake my head. "You were screaming at me!" We both chuckle and his cheeks turn pink because he knows I'm right.

Peter straightens and scoots so we are staring into each other's eyes. "I promise to try my best to not be annoying or yell at you over the comms."

"And I promise to do my best not to hang up on you. But you have to listen when I tell you to quiet down."

"I swear it." Peter pulls my hands, drawing me in and pressing his lips against mine. I kiss him back without hesitation.

The next day, the house is quiet. Both kids are lying about lazily, working on projects or listening to music or playing video games. Peter's been in his office working and after a few hours, I decide to check in on him knowing we have things to discuss today about our future and test results to go over.

Peter doesn't say anything as I crack open the office door, slip in, and take a seat in one of the cushioned chairs. I wait as he shuffles through papers, producing three stacks. When he finally looks up, he hands me a pen.

I take it, giving him a curious look. "Are we practicing my autograph today?" I laugh, but Peter is all business, his face barely twitching from his "professor" seriousness.

"There are some forms we need to update." He settles into his seat and clears his throat. "We need to update our life insurance policy, our will..." he lists.

I nod absently. "Do we really need to update anything? We just recently went over all this with the lawyer."

Peter smiles softly. "It's just to make sure we have things in order if—" He coughs, not wanting to say what we are both currently thinking.

If something goes wrong... if Jane doesn't make it back... if she disappears off the planet. A small smirk tugs at the corner of my mouth at his last thought. It seems Max has gotten into his head too.

"Okay. It would be good to make sure we didn't miss anything. You know, just in case."

Peter's head bobs once as he flips through the packet.

I've watched all the superhero movies with Max, and mostly, they've all survived and thrived. But they were also different from me; skilled, trained, specialized doctors to care for them, and most had money to take care of expenses and equipment. Me? A mom with two kids and a husband? I could leave them behind with nothing if I make one wrong move. The thought makes my chest tighten and my vision blurs with tears.

"I realize that I've been a bit naïve about this whole thing," I admit. "Although I have thought most of this through, there are certain aspects—certain consequences—that are beginning to sit heavier on me. After the other night..." I sigh, pushing my hair back from my face. "I know I need to consider the gray areas, too. Not just the black and white."

Oh, Jane. "This is just a precaution."

"We can't know that. We are both thinking the same thing," I argue. "This whole thing is dangerous. If I end up hurt or in the hospital or..." I sigh. "We need to know that everyone can still get by." I lick my lower lip and lean forward. "And what do we tell the hospital if I ever get taken there? One look at me and they'll be asking a thousand questions."

"We can discuss that. Figure out how to explain it."

"What will you say?" I snap. "Oh, my wife enjoys a good role-play as much as the others in this town?"

Peter scoffs, but quickly tries to cover it up with a cough again. "You could be a cosplayer or-or auditioning for a play! There's a million excuses we could come up with, but we could also just tell them the truth." At my eye roll he says, "You did say you didn't want to hide."

I nod, biting my lower lip so hard I can taste the copper of blood on my tongue. "There's suddenly so much we need to figure out."

"Now, where have I heard that before?" Peter smiles, raising his brows teasingly. Drawing the papers toward himself, he flips through to place a post-it note on one sheet. He jots a few words, then closes the packet. "We can make a list. Work through each together." Peter reaches over the desk, palm up, waiting for my hand. I slip my hand into his. "Right now, let's finish this paperwork. I'll note any other concerns to discuss and we will circle back. Okay?" I nod, releasing his hand and settling back into my seat.

After making a few more changes and reviewing insurance and finances, Peter withdraws lab results. By this point, Max found his way into the office and has been laying on the floor reading a comic book. As Peter mentions something about supercells, Max perks, shoving to his feet to include himself in the conversation.

"Noah and I have been running some tests on the initial blood we took," he begins. "From what we can see, your blood cells are oddly formed and colored compared to regular cells," Peter explains, sliding two pictures before me. One shows red, pillowy donut-shaped circles. Basic blood cells. The other image appears alien, with bluish tinted donuts mixed with some that seem to be wrapped in a hazy gauze.

"What's this?" I point to a few speckled patches in the photo of the regular cells. It looks like tiny grains of rice.

"Platelets." I glance at him because I don't know what that means. He gins, leaning forward and using his hands to explain further. "When your blood cells are forming in your marrow, they separate into two stems; lymphoid and myeloid. Basically, both stems result in red and white blood cells for the body to use in different ways."

I nod, doing my best to follow him, but biology was never a strong subject for me. "Everyone has white and red cells *and* platelets?"

"Yes. The platelets come from the myeloid stem, which is also in charge of making red blood cells, among other things," he says with a wave of his hands. "Most of the time, platelets are inactive, waiting for a cell to call out for help." He looks at Max, then me, to ensure we are still on the same page. "When the platelets get a signal for help, they travel through the body to the damaged vessel and transform into an active state, latching on to help."

"Cool." Max giggles.

"You have platelets, too," Peter tells me. "They're just modified." He points to the grainy rice area.

I squint at the image, hoping if I stare hard enough, it will become clear. "Modified how?"

This alien image shows similar clusters, but they're ominous between the bluish haze.

"Your platelets are waiting for a signal, too, but they're in an active state at all times." Pointing his pen at a large clutter with little tentacles sprouting from each cell, he continues, "These are in active form, ready to attach to a broken vessel, but none of your vessels need their aid, or it they do, like this one"—he moves his pen across the page to a cell slightly less blue with no haze—"they don't just attach themselves, they *devour* it."

My jaw drops. "Devour? Instead of latching on and fixing any broken cells, you're saying these platelets, *my platelets,* are destroying them?"

His head sways. "Not destroy. Devour." Peter licks his lips, then raises his hand to demonstrate. "They transform themselves around the broken vessel and take its place." He cups one hand over the other. "Your platelets take the cell's place and fill its role." Dropping the covered hand, Peter grins with a single raised fist. "Mutation in an instant," he concludes, eyes twinkling with new discovery, sitting with his fist hovering as if waiting for a first bump to congratulate him.

I deflate into my chair, trying to wrap my head around the fact that my cells are just devouring each other. No big deal, right? I shouldn't freak out, but my heart is picking up speed and I feel like I need to clean something or fold laundry or anything to occupy my hands.

"And you're sure about this? How can you know for sure that's what they're doing?" I wonder knowing between teaching, home life, and now our super life, there isn't much time left to sit around staring at cells.

"Noah—Dr. Chandra—and I recorded the cells over a forty-eight hour period. We took turns checking in on the samples."

"Recorded? How?"

Peter's gaze flickers to Max, then to the stack of papers before him. "We... uh... *borrowed* one of the microscopes from the genetics lab and set it up in my office. It has a camera feature that will capture footage or images while in use."

"Uh-huh," I muse, narrowing my gaze.

"It was the easiest way for us to observe how the cells interacted with each other and changed over a short period of time. Noah said no one was using them right now anyway, so they wouldn't be missed. It was fascinating to watch, actually," he chirped, smiling.

I glance at Max who is nodding. A wide-grin plastered on his face as he takes in the images before us. "This is really exciting," he remarks. "This is like Basic Superhero 101: Cell Mutation. It's in all the movies!"

With an exhale, I puff my cheeks. "And what does all this mean? What's so important about this specifically?"

"Our bodies are always creating cells, like a machine keeping up with production. The blue compound they gave us to study was rumored to be a crucial component to fix the powerhouse where individual's systems were compromised. Auto-immune diseases. Cancer." He ticks off examples on his hand. "This compound is... was... supposed to be the key to curing endless diseases."

"But I wasn't sick."

"Right." Peter points a finger at me as if the thought just occurred to him, too. He leafs through a pile of papers, then withdraws a second image of blue cells. This one looks as though it is more aglow than the first. "Dr. Chandra and I believe what is happening to you is the compound is finding holes in your system, or areas that could be, well... enhanced." He clears his throat at my stare. "The compound is mutating to make certain areas stronger. Make them better, more efficient."

"Make me super." I touch the image. It appears similar to the first, except these cells appear thicker.

Peter's head bobs. "Making you super." He pauses, letting the words sink in. "This is the same blood, days after natural mutation from the first image."

"And the color?"

"A side-effect of the compound." Peter shrugs.

I point to the little blue donuts again. "And this hazy barrier here?"

Peter leans forward to see what I'm pointing at, then eases back. "From what we surmise, those are cells in the process of transformation from platelet to red blood cell. The haze is like a protective barrier."

I stare at him and blink because this all makes my head spin.

"Think of those platelets as a fetus and the haze a type of womb to keep it safe while growing and shaping. This one here," he says, pointing his pen to a bright blue one with a comet-like tail trailing it. "This one is shedding the barrier and taking the final steps to becoming a red, or in your case, blue cell."

Picking up the image, I scrutinize it. "It is kind of beautiful," I say softly after a moment.

Max shifts to look over my arm at the image and nods in agreement. "It's really cool."

"These platelets are filling in gaps in my programming?"

Peter nods.

"And by doing so, it's giving my body a boost in certain areas, enhancing what is already there, and making me super. Therefore I can read minds... am stronger...?"

"There are more tests to run to confirm all of that, but yes. That is my conclusion so far."

"And for more tests you need...?"

Max perks, standing and pacing in the small space. "We will need a device to record the amount of energy exerted from your super strength, and perhaps some probes to read your mindwaves while you're listening to thoughts—"

"None of those things exist in this universe," I tell Max, then look at Peter. "Right?"

He scratches the back of his neck. "None that I'm aware of."

Max deflates. "Oh, well, what are you going to do then if this kind of equipment isn't invented in this realm yet?"

I chuckle as quietly as I can because my soft-hearted boy is trying so hard to be helpful in his own way. In his mind, because I have powers in this world, it means the stories from his comics are real, too. In a way...

Peter takes a post-it note and begins scribbling a list. "I'll need more blood to work with. If I can examine the growth and change from the first sample, I can understand it better. Even after letting it mutate on its own, it was outside the body. I'll take more blood and see how it has changed internally. It would be good to schedule an MRI to examine your brain and organs, too. A psych test as well."

I scoff. "A psych test?"

Peter's eyes shift uncomfortably between Max and I. "Y-yes," he stammers. "Strictly routine for any experiment, especially one that is tested on humans. We need to keep it between the few of us though, since the company did not approve human tests."

"And how do we go about getting an MRI without telling everyone what you're looking for?"

"I have some friends at the hospital..."

"Peter, they're not going to just let you walk in and schedule an MRI without cause."

He exhales sharply. "Well, let me see what I can collect in the labs. I'm sure Noah has some connections in other medical departments—"

"And what about the company that provided the compound? Haven't they been inquiring about your progress and findings so far? Do they know you took it from the lab? Do they know it's gone and—"

"Jane." Peter stops me. "Obviously I didn't tell them all of this." He sighs, rubbing his hands down his face. "I wasn't supposed to remove it from the lab. I'm not supposed to remove *any* experiments from the lab."

"Then why did you?" I snap.

"I don't know." He tosses his hands up. "The package came in late and I was heading out the door. I just shoved it into my bag not thinking about what it was. When I got home and finally opened it and saw what it was, I put it in the fridge to take back as soon as I could. Look," he continues, leaning forward. "It doesn't matter why or whatever because it all happened and mistakes were made... I don't know what I was thinking."

"This was part of a research grant, right?" I inquire. Peter nods. "So wasn't there a whole team assigned to this project?"

"Technically, yes. I was in the process of selecting students to help with the research, but none had been notified yet. I'll have to assign them something this week or the company will be wondering why we are sitting on the project." He shakes his head. "It's fine. We will use the tests we've already ran, gather new blood, and let the students run their sequences with those."

"And when the students ask why they're running tests on blood and not the compound itself...?"

Peter closes his eyes, pinching the bridge of his nose. "I'll tell them it's from the animal testing phase. It's not unheard of for professors to begin the project and have students jump in to assist later."

Silence builds between us. Max returned to his comic, laying on the floor quietly. I let my mind wander, trilling over the information we have so far.

"What do we know about this company?"

Peter leans his elbows on the table and continues, "They're based in Central Asia, so most communication has been through email. I have told them we are preparing samples, but they won't be coming to the lab for weeks, if at all, I'd imagine." Peter taps his pen against the desk, staring at the paperwork before him. "The MSAD corp is new to us, but from what I've read about them, they're extremely meticulous. They'll be asking harder questions soon. We just need to be prepared to answer them."

"MSAD? What does that even stand for?"

"Medical and Science of Alien Discovery," Max states, and I shoot him a curious—and shocked—stare. "What?"

"How do you know that?" Peter asks.

"I really like superhero stuff, remember?"

I rub my arms, feeling a chill in the air. "That explains a lot, I suppose. If they're thinking this is some alien compound, that does what they believe it to do, they'd be the richest people in the entire world."

Max blows a raspberry. "More like the universe!"

Cheyanne's shadow fills the doorway. "What's going on?" She crosses her arms over her chest, looking between the three of us.

"Mom has alien blood! Look!" Max shoots to his feet, snatching the photo of the blue cells and shoving in front of Chayanne. "It's so cool."

She grimaces. "Gross." Dropping her arms, she let out a weighted sigh. "Can I go to Megan's for dinner?"

"It's family movie night," Max whines, his grin dropping in disappointment. *I spent hours picking out our movie.* His heartbreak reaches my mind.

"He's right," I tell Cheyanne. "And since when are you and Megan on speaking terms again?"

Cheyanne scrunches her nose in frustration. "Friends can make up. Plus, we have this presentation for Spanish due on Tuesday."

I narrow my gaze at her. *Plus, I want my sweater back,* Cheyenne grumblers internally.

"Fine. Do you need a ride?"

Cheyanne sways her head. "She's leaving some church thing and said she can pick me up. Since *she* has her license already."

I pretend not to notice that her upper lip twitches into a snarl.

Peter clears his throat. I glance at him and see a single brow raised. *We could use an extra driver...* he prompts. Letting out a heavy sigh, I face Cheyanne and stare at her.

"What?" she scowls. *Why is she looking at me like that?*

"Okay," I huff.

Cheyanne slumps. "Okay, what?"

"You can get your license."

"Wait. Really?" Cheyanne straightens, letting her gaze shift between

Peter and I.

I side-eye Peter. "Your father thinks you're ready." I return to hold Cheyanne's gaze. "And I have to say, it would be good to have an extra driver around," I conclude.

Cheyenne's lips pull into a toothy grin. "I already have my permit, so taking the licensing test wouldn't take more than an afternoon appointment."

I blink rapidly. *Permit?* "How do you have your permit already?"

"It's an elective course, mom." She rolls her eyes, then withdraws her phone. Her nails tap against the screen as she speaks. "You signed the form letting me take it last semester, but when the final driving test came, you said you didn't think I was ready. So, I have my permit, but never got to do the licensing final."

Max coughs. "You ran over the neighbor's cat."

"Shut up, chimp."

"Twice," Max adds, before ducking behind my chair to avoid the slashing hand of his sister.

"Enough," I command, raising my hand to silence them. "Sign up for the test, please. I'll sign whatever forms needed. Go to Megan's for dinner, but be home before ten."

Cheyanne purses her lips to contain a smile, then breezes out of the room.

"Was that a mistake?" I wonder, but a teasing grin is on my face.

Peter chuckles. "Probably. We should advise the neighbors to keep their animals inside for a while, though."

CHAPTER 13

Max is yelling from the living room for me to hurry. He's preparing the movie and I'm on popcorn duty.

"Two minutes," I holler, checking my phone I left charging on the counter. An email notification appears and I click to open it. It's from Rebecca about the upcoming PTA elections. The entire committee is voted on once a year. Normally we never worry about opponents because no one has been brave enough to stand against Rebecca, but perhaps this year will be different.

The microwave chimes and it's enough to bring me back. I set my phone down, thinking that maybe I could run for vice president this year, or even secretary. There's never been a vice president in the last few years as Rebecca states she didn't believe the PTA needed one, but with how the parents reacted to my recent suggestions, maybe it was finally time to ring in a second-in-command.

I dump the popcorn into the large bowl and head to the living room. The TV isn't playing the opening of a movie, though; the news is on. Both Peter and Max are staring at the screen.

"Did something happen?" I wonder, setting the bowl down and snuggling next to Peter on the couch.

Peter shushes me, gesturing to the TV where the local news station is on.

"... it is quite unbelievable." A male news anchor chuckles, his blond hair held in a perfect swoosh, and his black-framed glasses give his serious features a softer look.

"Why are we—" I try to inquire as we rarely watch the local station unless it's snowing and the kids are hoping for school closures. Peter shushes me, though. I huff, rolling my eyes, but focus back on whatever story is going on in the community.

"Well, what do you think, Charles?" The woman cohosting asks, leaning her petite elbows on the glass table before her. She tucks a perfect ginger curl behind her ear.

Charles leans back in his seat. "I think someone is playing a prank."

"What are they—" I start, but Peter shushes me again. Our town only has one local news station, being how compact we are, but they never fail to find the juiciest gossip around the neighborhoods.

"For those just tuning in, Blaire and I are discussing the robbery that happened last night on Elmont Ave."

The camera pans out as Blaire continues. "Police arrested two men who had broken into a residence on Elmont. Both men claim they weren't apprehended by local authorities alone, though."

"The suspects state that a plus-sized woman wearing some sort of Halloween costume was on the scene first." Charles chuckles, adjusting his glasses.

"A masked vigilante," Blaire corrects.

"Mom!" Max shuffles on his knees to face me. "They're talking about *you*!"

I glance at him, then back at the screen because he is absolutely right. My pulse quickens and the air in the room grows thick. *Do they know who I am?*

"Whoever this woman is," Charles rolls his eyes and smirks. "She is responsible for helping police capture the robbers, who authorities now believe have been leading the string of break-ins over the last six months."

"Holy shit," Peter blurts. Max giggles, but clamps his mouth shut when I see Peter shoot him a threatening glare. "Max is right, isn't he? They're talking about you?"

I nod, not taking my eyes off the TV. The reporters are still talking about the case, recalling items that were stolen over the last few months before the screen fills with mug-shots of the two men. A flash of the evening floods my mind. It is definitely the men I saw. They *are* 100 percent talking about me. I cover my mouth with my hand.

This is what I wanted. I have to remind myself of this because my stomach is churning and I feel like I may vomit.

"Brandon Rameriz, twenty-eight, will more than likely be let off easy. This is his first offense," Blaire continues. "While Jason Monroe, thirty-nine... I'm sure some of you may recognize him. He's been *featured* on our station before. This isn't his first offense, by far, and we hope they give him a full sentence. In our county that would mean up to ten years in prison."

"Let's hope for more than that," Charles interrupts. "Jason Monroe has been on our local watch list for, not only breaking and entering, but carjacking, attempted arson, and more. It's about time we finally brought him in. Don't you think, Blaire?"

The news anchor flashes her perfect teeth. "Oh, I do, Charles. Thanks go to the masked woman who helped the police catch the two bandits."

"P.S. Jane," Charles chimes. Blaire side-eyes him, then glances at the notes on the desk. "That's what the men said was on her costume."

"It sounds like it was a supersuit." Blaire tilts her head and laughs once.

"Whatever she was wearing," he waves her off. "We all want to know who she is and if we will ever see our very own local super again. Police are actively looking for this new superhero and urge anyone with information to contact the department."

"Let's hope they're looking to give her a medal," Blaire mocks.

Charles chuckles. "More like an interrogation." Blaire's eyebrows raise. "We contacted local police Chief Arnold Brown for a statement. He claims that while this hero's intentions were good, they'd rather handle issues on their own." The camera pans to a single shot of Charles, zooming in slowly as he speaks. "If this woman involves herself in crime around town, there's no telling if—or when—she may get injured or unintentionally tamper with a scene."

"If you ask me, the Chief sounds leery of this super." The camera flashes to Blaire, then zooms out to show both anchors.

"As he should be."

"Well, in my opinion, she's only trying to help. We can't fault her for wanting to assist our community. Can we?"

"I disagree. We aren't living in a movie. Real people—our town folks and neighbors—could seriously be hurt by her actions. Or worse."

Blaire nods in agreement. "That's true, but, let's see what the people say." She stares into the camera as it zooms in on her. "Do you believe P.S. Jane should continue being a hero, or step down and let officials handle our community? Send us a text at—"

I click the TV off and stare at the black screen.

"You're famous!" Max whispers, laying his head on my lap.

My eye is twitching with uncertainty and nerves, but I manage a half-smile as I glance at Max. His eyes are twinkling with enthusiasm, and a cheerful grin takes over his features. *This is so cool!* he thinks.

Peter is staring at me, unsure of what move he should make. *I should ask if she's okay. No. Let her be. She'll come to me if she needs help. Is she processing this? Why is she so quiet? I should ask...* He blinks as my sight lands on him.

This is what I wanted. Right? This is it. This is the moment it all becomes reality. I'm chewing on my bottom lip, tearing at the chapped skin. Peter observes me with a look of sympathy, but he shouldn't. This is exactly what I wanted… right?

I take a deep inhale, exhaling slowly through my nose. "This is happening how it should," I say, almost as if reassuring myself. "I wanted to help—I *want* to help. This is my purpose. It's just… I definitely didn't think this whole publicity thing through." I laugh lightly and Peter smiles.

Peter wraps an arm around me. "I tried to warn you," he teases. "Plus, you've watched all these super movies with Max. You knew eventually your name would get out there. Wasn't that the point?" I tilt my head to stare at him. "Being a superhero means having your face plastered on the news, and all over the internet. It's going to be part of the gig." He draws me close, placing a kiss on my head. "Maybe you'll get an action figure." Peter's tone is tinged with sarcasm.

I snort. "Can you imagine a P.S. Jane action figure?"

"I'd buy the shit out of that!" Max interrupts, scooting into the corner of the couch and drawing a blanket over himself.

"Language," Peter and I both say at the same time. Max shrugs, stuffing a fist full of popcorn into his mouth with one hand, while the other is working the DVD remote. The TV clicks back on, but this time movie previews fill the screen.

"Just remember," Peter says quietly. "We're all here to support you; mask on or off."

CHAPTER 14

My stomach is growling so loudly I can barely focus on the police scanner. I give into the annoyance and step from the van, making my way to the familiar hot dog cart around the corner.

"One hot dog with ketchup, please," I say to the man. He glances at me, then does a double take.

Holy shit, he thinks. "If it isn't our very own super." He chuckles, withdrawing a steamy dog from the convection belt. "Heard your story on the news the other day and I thought to myself, 'That's the comic convention lady!'" Setting the dog in the bun, he hands me the paper plate. "But don't worry," he leans in to whisper. "Your secret is safe with me."

"T-Thanks." I take the hot dog, squeezing the offered ketchup onto it. Thrusting him a five-dollar bill, he holds up a hand to stop me. "It's $5, right?"

His head sways. "Police and superheroes eat free after nine."

I clench the bill into my fist. "Oh, but I—"

"Just take the hot dog and do some good out there. You hear?"

I nod, lifting the hot dog in a thanks and turn.

"Stay safe out there, P.S. Jane," he calls as I round the corner.

When I'm tucked back into the van, I eat the hot dog in four bites. It's been quiet on the scanner, but I still try to chew quietly so I can hear if anything comes through. Peter's not in my ear at the moment, and it feels too silent. I'm tempted to turn on the radio for some background noise, but then the scanner buzzes alive.

"Officer Richard, what's your twenty?"

"Patrol. East Side."

"Copy. We have a 10-42 on the corner of East Baseline and Hamilton."

"10-4."

I scan my notebook of the local codes. Malicious mischief and vandalism. Clicking on the Bluetooth, I wait for Peter to answer.

"Hey, how's it going?" Peter yawns.

With a smile, I turn the key in the ignition. "Great. There's a possible vandalism call I'm going to check out. I'm about five minutes away."

"Vandalism?" Peter sighs. "It's probably some teenagers tagging signs."

"Who cares? It's something! Maybe I can scare some sense into them." I pull out of the parking lot and head left. "Use my mom voice and power of persuasion."

"None of your abilities include persuasion, Jane."

I click my tongue at him. "When I had Cheyanne, it was gifted to me."

Peter chuckles. "Okay. Okay. Be safe. I'll be on the line if you need me."

"Copy that," I reply, hitting the blinker and turning down East Baseline.

The road is straight and filled with four-way stops, but it's dark and lined with thick trees. In the past, there have been many late-night accidents on this road as drivers barely stop to actually look at the crossroads. Some don't even bother stopping at all. This late, there aren't many cars on the road, but I still take my time at every sign, looking both ways before proceeding forward. As I approach Hamilton, I pull into the dark parking lot of a mini-mart that has been closed for years. They boarded the windows, but glass sparkles from the concrete against my headlights as I find a dark corner.

Slipping from the van, I tiptoe to the street, using the telephone poles as cover. There's a large shrub at the intersection, and I duck behind it, listening for any sounds of disturbance. I'm met with only the songs of the crickets.

"It's quiet," I tell Peter, standing and searching the area. "I don't see anyone."

"Whoever it was is probably long gone by now," he replies and the sound of keys tapping fills the silence.

"Perhaps," I muse, stepping from my cover to stand on the corner. Then I notice it. A stop sign bent at an odd angel. It's halfway to the ground, looking as though someone took a bat to it. If any cars come by, they'd run through it. It's an accident waiting to happen. "A stop sign is down."

Peter doesn't respond, though. I take a quick glance around before stretching out my arms.

"Hey!" a male voice shouts. I yelp at the sudden boom in the silence and spin on my heels to find a man wearing an athletic suit with reflective tape on it. He nods to the pole. "I've called the cops they—" he jogs across the street, but noticing my outfit pauses halfway. A snort escapes him.

I purse my lips and glance at the starry sky as I tune into his thoughts. *What the hell... Oh, shit! This is...*

"P.S. Jane," I finish his thought with a smirk. "Yes. That's me. I heard the call about the vandalism. Was that you?"

"Oh, no. I didn't... I saw some kids when I ran by the first time. Cops said they'd send someone, but I wasn't going to wait around," he explains.

"By the first time? You run this road often?"

He nods. "Every night. Down to Vermont Street and back. Good for the health," he snarks, eyes taking me in. With a shake of his head, he takes two steps forward and scoffs. "You know, I called this into the *cops*, not some wannabe housewife hero." Withdrawing a small water bottle from the belt at his waist, he takes a long chug. When he's done, he wipes the droplets from his mouth with the back of his palm.

"I'm not some—" I huff.

"Leave it to the real heroes, *P.S. Jane,*" he says my name mockingly and begins to walk backwards. A car passes by slowly. I feel their gaze on me as they drift through the intersection, without stopping, and continue on their way.

"Asshole," I groan, watching the man continue his nightly run and disappear into the night. He must live in the neighborhood at the end of Hamilton. There's an elementary school and a cozy cul-de-sac with swanky homes he's probably jogging toward right now.

"Well, that was weird," Peter chuckles into the phone.

Turning back to the sign, I assess it once again. "Yeah. Didn't seem too happy with me being here. I bet he voted 'no' on the local station's stupid poll." Peter laughs again, and I can't help but smile. "Alright, Jane. It's go time."

I drop into a half-squat under the sign and grip the pole with both hands. With a single inhale, I thrust the pole away from me. It bends up, up, up and then is too far forward.

"Crap."

"What's wrong?" Peter perks.

I adjust my mask and reposition myself on the other side of the sign. "Nothing. I just bent it too far." Peter chuckles.

This time, I focus my attention on using *less* strength and ease the sign as straight as I can. As I'm adjusting it, shoving the pole deeper into the ground and kicking dirt in the enlarged hole, a police car siren chirps behind me.

"Double crap." I freeze. Peter is talking to me, but I shush him. "Police are here." I turn, giving an awkward wave to the officer exiting the vehicle. "Just one officer. Should be okay."

The officer takes cautious steps toward me, hand at the ready where his weapon is holstered. His eyes flicker over me, taking in my skin tight suit.

"Evening officer," I say cheerfully. "I found this sign bent and was just straightening it before any accidents happened."

His eyebrows lift. "We had a call about vandalism."

"The man who called it in ran that way," I say pointing down the road. The officer glances over his shoulder, then focuses on me again. "But I didn't see who did the vandalizing." I shrug. "This pole looked as though it took a beating, though. No worries, I worked it back into place." I knock my knuckles against the sign, making a *ting* noise.

"Huh." His hands relax as he scratches his chin. "And you just *bent* this back? By yourself?"

I nod. "I'm stronger than I look."

"Right." He shifts his weight to one foot. "And you are?"

"P.S. Jane." I point to my suit where the letters are stitched. "Perhaps you've heard of me?" Now I'm sounding cocky, and I tell myself to ease up.

The officer reaches for the radio on his shoulder. Without taking his eyes off me, he calls into dispatch. "Officer Richards to dispatch."

"This is dispatch." I hear the familiar female voice respond.

"I'm at the 10-42. Possibly a 10-41. Female. Wearing a supersuit."

There's a long pause on the radio. "Copy. Did you say supersuit?"

"Peter," I whisper harshly. "What's a 10-41?"

Typing comes through the device in my ear. "Um," he chuckles, "a drunk."

I sigh. "Look, Officer Richards. I'm not drunk or causing mischief. I heard the call for possible vandalism and came here to check on it."

"Uh-huh, and we got a call just seconds ago claiming a suspicious woman was at the very scene where the vandalism happened."

I narrow my gaze at the darkened street knowing that the ass called the cops again. On me! "Strange. It's just me!" I laugh half-heartedly.

"Jane..." Peter's worried tone comes through. I take a breath to calm my growing nerves. This cop better not be here to arrest me.

"What did you say your name was?" he asks, brows drawn in.

I point to my suit for the second time. "P.S. Jane."

"She's calling herself P.S. Jane," he radios.

"That's the woman from the news the other night," dispatch says.

"You know about her?" His posture relaxes and a look of surprise crosses his face.

His radio crackles before dispatch comes back. "She helped capture the two men that were part of the string of burglaries. She must be the woman Mr. Clark called about."

"Jane," Peter whispers. "Everything okay?"

"I think so."

"Okay, *P.S. Jane*," Officer Richard snarks. "You think you're some superhero?" I flicker my gaze from him to the ground. I can hear his internal voice chuckling at this whole situation. "You say you bent this sign back. Prove it." His hands rest on his hips as he watches. It's obvious he doesn't believe me with the smug smile on his face. Another vote of 'no' for the local station.

"You want me to... *re-bend* the pole?" I hope this isn't a trap to get me to show that I vandalized the sign in the first place or something sneaky. He nods once, gesturing to the stop sign. I look at it. There's still a crease where it was originally bent, but if I bend it there again, it may snap in two. Instead, I reach below the indent, squatting to ensure I lift with my legs, and yank the whole sign out of the ground in a single grunt.

"What the fu—"

"I did tell you," I say, shoving it back into the ground behind the original hole. "I'm stronger than I look."

Another car drifts by. This time, they pause at the stop sign before proceeding. I cheer internally at a successful job. Brushing the invisible grime from my hands, I watch the officer. He's examining the pole, eyeing me cautiously.

"I should probably bring you into the station. The Chief has been in a tizzy over the fact that we have a so-called *super* in town," he finally says. There's an awkward pause as he shifts his balance between his feet. Then, he's shaking his head and laughing. "What has this world come to? Curvy women dressing up to save the day like some sort of freaky fetish."

I clear my throat. "Ex-excuse me?" *I'm right here prick.*

"Look," he begins, scratching his nose. "I'm all for people helping out the community. And this"—he gestures to the sign—"was helpful. It would have taken at least a week to get a crew out to replace this sign." The officer glances around. "In that time, there could have been a few accidents."

"Right," I drawl, narrowing my gaze in confusion. *Where is he going with this?* I tune into his thoughts, trying to gauge his next move.

This is insane. If I bring her in, they're just going to waste their time questioning her. It's just a sign. She saved me the hassle of doing the paperwork and contacting—

"It *is* just a sign," I reiterate with a shrug. Officer Richard's blinks at me, stunned.

"I... uh... yes. Yes, it is." He sniffs, looping his thumbs into his belt. "Look, thank you for the help tonight..."

"P.S. Jane."

"Right. P.S. Jane. But this should only be a one time thing."

"One time," I repeat.

He nods. "I highly suggest you *not* interfere with police business." Stepping toward the vehicle, he opens the door, leaning his arm on the window. "I'm going to let this slide. This time. But if I find you interfering again, I'll have no choice but to bring you to the station."

"What about your boss?" I wonder. Max would tell me to offer to rough him up so the chief thinks I escaped capture or something. I bite my tongue to stifle a laugh as the image of me punching the officer in the nose flashes in my mind. Now that would get me arrested for sure!

"This one's on me." With a wink, he slides into the driver's seat. I watch as he closes the door and begins to drive away from the roadside. The police car eases by, stopping before me. The passenger window rolls down.

"And P.S. Jane?" he says, then smiles. "Thanks for fixing the sign." He tips his head then leaves me standing on the edge of the road a bit bewildered.

Officer Richards could have easily cuffed me and brought me into the station. I could have been stuck answering questions about my power and how I knew what he was thinking, but instead, he let me go. I'm not really sure why. Perhaps he'd rather not have a potentially crazed woman in his car. Maybe he believes they'd make fun of him at the station if he told them he believed me. Whatever the officer's reasons were, I can't help but silently thank him for letting me off with a *little* warning... a suggestion, as he said. One I do not intend to heed.

CHAPTER 15

U p early, I made brownies from a box mix I had in the pantry and plated them for the PTA meeting. Today is the day we discuss the vote for the new president. I'm eager to put my name down for a role this time. Whether that be vice president or secretary, I wasn't sure, but I know I want to be more involved after the response of the previous meeting.

I'm the first one at the meeting, again, and I set the tray of brownies in the center of the table along with a stack of paper napkins. Sitting at my usual spot, I sip my Starbucks while I wait. It doesn't take long before I hear Rebecca's thoughts running through my mind and the clack of her heels against the tile hall.

*Of course they will let me continue being president. No one else would dare run against me. And if anyone—*her steps halt. "Jane. Hello," she says.

As I pivot to reply, I notice her pursed lips and narrow gaze. "Afternoon, Rebecca. How are you?"

She taps her nail against her bag before continuing to her seat. "Wonderful." *Life is fucking dandy,* her internal thoughts spit. Her eyes zero in on the brownies. "What are these?"

"Oh, just a little treat for everyone. I had some extra time today, so I whipped up a batch before the meeting," I tell her proudly. "Help yourself to one."

"No, thank you. I don't like sweets." *Damn, those look good,* she thinks. Rebecca blinks, then turns her attention to her bag. Unpacking clipboards and folders, she does her best to ignore me while I sip my coffee. The rest of the PTA group arrives minutes later, and the brownies are devoured.

"Okay everyone," Rebecca begins, smiling her perfect grin at us. "Let's begin the meeting today. There are only a few matters to discuss before we break into groups to tackle the upcoming fundraisers. Foremost, the PTA elections." She flips her inky hair over her shoulder. "Let's make a list of who would like to be acknowledged on the ballot this year. I already put my name down." She laughs once. "Is anyone interested in the treasury position besides Michael?"

No one raises their hand.

"Splendid." Rebecca jots his name down. "And secretary?"

Stacy's hand shoots up followed by Gina, another mom who has been gunning for the position for two turns. Rebecca writes their names down with a nod.

"Okay, that's that."

"Uh, Rebecca? Aren't you going to ask if anyone wants the vice president or president position?" All eyes turn to me.

Rebecca glares. "We've never had a vice president, Jane. You know this." *Bitch.*

"Maybe we need one."

Rebecca scoffs. "Why? We are doing just fine without one." *Shut up, Jane.*

"Okay, then I'd like to put my name down for president." I straighten in my chair, folding my hands on the table.

Rebecca's lips curl in and I swear the organic silk of her shirt just wrinkled. "*You* want to be considered for president?" she asks through her teeth.

"Yes. Yes, I do."

Her knuckles turn white as she grips the pen. Lynn is staring at me like I said the world is about to end. Perhaps it will once my name is on the list.

"Okay, Jane. *President nominee.* Anyone else?" Rebecca's glare darts around the table, but no one dares to raise their hand or look at her. *Fucking great. Not like she's going to win.* She writes my name down with a heavy hand. I can hear the paper practically tearing from here.

"I can't believe you did that," Lynn tells me once Rebecca has spouted off about the fundraisers.

I shoot a half-smile at Lynn, but my eyes are on Rebecca who may have a forced friendly smile on her perfect face, but internally is snarling and tearing me apart.

As everyone heads to the parking lot after the meeting, I wave at Lynn and pack up my notes. My notebook is full of ideas for not only the next season, but the next year as well. The desire to be a leader of the group only increases as the meeting progressed.

Slinging my purse over my shoulder with a victorious smile, I turn to head to my van.

"Still here, Jane? You're usually the first one to leave." Rebecca's voice gives me pause. It's oddly smooth and friendly, a tone I don't believe I've ever heard from her.

I rotate to face her. "A few parents wanted to run ideas by me, so I jotted down their thoughts." I raise the notebook in my hand at her.

She smiles and clicks her tongue. "Our very own Jane, rising to the occasion." *Seriously, why is everyone suddenly obsessed with her?*

"Um, yeah. Right." I shift my purse on my arm. "Well, I should go. I need to pick up groceries before I get Max."

"I'll walk with you." Rebecca grabs her satchel, swinging her keys on her finger.

I hesitate. Either Rebecca has become possessed by some godly spirit, or she's actually trying to be nice to me. I'm suspicious either way.

"Sure."

We walk in silence through the school hall. It's not until we exit the front door and down the pathway to the lot that Rebecca takes a deep breath.

"It's such a gorgeous day. This entire season has been wonderful, really. If the weather holds like this, it will be perfect for the upcoming events," Rebecca chats casually.

"That's true."

"You know, Jane. I'm surprised you volunteered your name for the vice president's position."

"You mean president," I correct.

She flashes her teeth. "Right. Well, we've never had a vice president in the past." She jingles her keys, then glances at me continuing to ignore the fact that *she* wrote my name down beside her for the leadership position. "You're usually not one to actively volunteer for stuff," she adds, and I flash her an annoyed smile. "No offense, but it's true. Recently, there's been something different about you, though." Rebecca slows as we approach her black sedan.

"I feel different," I tell her with a shrug.

She must be on medication. Finally, I knew she needed it. I hear her think and chew on my bottom lip to keep from snarling at her. Tired of her rude banter, I force myself to close off the connection to her mind.

Rebecca opens the driver door and pauses, studying me. "If you're serious about running as my second-in-command—"

PRESIDENT, I shout in my mind.

"Then we should meet for coffee later this week. Run our ideas by each other. See if we are on the same page."

"S-sure," I stammer, taken aback by this change of character.

"I'll text you," she says, sliding into the car.

I stare, stepping away as she pulls out of the space. Rebecca waves, flashing me a friendly smile before disappearing around the corner.

"What the fuck just happened?" I exhale sharply, shaking the weird feeling that's taken over my body. It's like a Spidey sense, some tingle that's telling me to pay attention to what's in front of me, to find the small, out-of-place detail.

CHAPTER 16

R ebecca and I have been civil the last few days, and Lynn is suspicious of the new friendly demeanor after hearing we had coffee once outside of PTA hours.

"There's no way she's not after something," Lynn says, sipping her coffee. I asked her to stop by to talk about the PTA events we were leading and to catch up. "If I were you, I'd be careful what I tell her. She could use anything you say against you to boot you from the PTA election." She pops a bite of blueberry muffin into her mouth, brushing the crumbs from her blouse.

With a sigh, I lean against the counter. "You're probably right. But really, who would believe her anyway?"

"Enough about Rebecca. Have you been watching the story of that local super?"

I blanch, feeling the blood drain from my face. "Uh, yeah. I've seen some stories about it." It's hard not to when it's the only real news that's happening in Brightwood in ages!

Lynn scoffs with a laugh. "This chick is on fire. I'd love to meet her." She lifts the mug to her lips, eyeing me curiously. "I'm sure she'd be a hoot at any party."

The room feels hot. I pick at my muffin, tuning into Lynn's thoughts. *There's only one Jane I know of,* she thinks.

"I wonder who she is," Lynn muses, then sets her mug down and stares at me. *P.S. Jane. It's not very original or identity-concealing.*

I drain the last of my coffee and turn to the sink, unable to look at her anymore. The whole family promised not to spill the secret, but if someone guesses, what am I supposed to do?

Setting my mug in the dishwasher, I hear, "I know it's you."

Turning on my heels, I face Lynn. "You can't tell anyone."

"Oh, my—" Lynn spits her coffee out. "I didn't even... You can... Holy shit!" It is only then I realize Lynn hadn't said her comment, but thought it and I've just outed myself.

I shush her. "You can't tell anyone. I'm not even supposed to tell you."

"What the hell, Jane! This is... this is crazy. *You're* crazy! You could get arrested for the shit you're doing! Damn, girl." She sways her head in disbelief, but her smile is in awe. "I knew something was up with you. You've been acting so strange and I couldn't put my finger on it. I thought maybe you got on some new medication or your sex life was just on fire lately."

"Lynn," I groan.

She holds up her hands. "All I know is that I had a feeling. And I was right. I was *so* frickin' right." Lynn slaps a palm on the counter. "Now, tell me everything."

Halfway through the explanation, we move to the living room to be more comfortable. The story was lengthy, and Lynn had a lot of questions, but we're on the same page.

"It's unbelievable," Lynn says after I conclude my story. "I mean, it's happening, and it's you, so it is believable, but I never imagined superpowers to be real."

"Me either." I sink into the couch.

Lynn leans forward, placing her elbows on her knees. "I want to help.

How do I get in the inner circle?"

I furrow my brows and chuckle. "It's just us, Lynn. No one else knows it's me."

"But they could. It wasn't hard for me to piece it together. Plus, your name... you practically told everyone who you are."

She's right and I exhale sharply. "I'm not trying to hide who I am. I'm not some Peter Parker or Superman trying to conceal myself. I am who I am. I'm not ashamed of it."

"So, then why don't you just interview with the local station? They'd be all over that shit and you know it."

I sigh. "I can't do that."

"Why not? That makes literally no sense. You don't want to hide yet here you are." Lynn gestures wildly at me. "Sitting on the couch, drinking coffee, talking about how you're *not* telling anyone who you are. That's kind of contradictory, isn't it?" She eyes me, sipping her coffee slowly with a knowing smirk.

"You're right," I admit. "I'll think—"

The kitchen door slams shut, startling both Lynn and I.

"Jane? We have a problem!" Peter shouts. I hear keys hit the counter and footsteps pound across the tile. "The lab is asking for more data and—" Peter enters the living room and notices Lynn. He falters, taking a step back and covering his mouth. "I-I didn't know we had company."

"It's fine, Peter. Lynn figured it all out on her own."

"Yeah, I want to be on the team," Lynn adds with a grin.

Peter shakes his head. "Um, that's great. But, Jane, we got an email from the supplier asking for more tests."

"What tests?"

"Tests I can't run on a *human* subject. Tests that I can only do with samples of the compound when it's isolated."

I shrug. "Just take some more blood. I don't mind."

"It's not that simple. They want to come and see the samples being tested."

"When are they coming?"

Peter scratches his chin. "Next week."

"Okay. Well. Shit." I groan. "We can... we can do this," I say, trying to sound as confident as I can.

Peter's nodding, but I can tell I already lost him in thought, coming up with options for us. "We need to tell them."

"No. Not yet," I argue.

Lynn interjects. "Why not, Jane? We just talked about how easy it will be for people to figure out it's *you*." She starts ticking off items on her fingers. "You said you don't want to hide. You're out there telling people *your name*. P.S. Jane. Why not just tell them you drank it? Fess up. What are they going to do, ask for it back?" Her face twists into a sarcastic smirk I can only imagine is meant to be a gesture telling me what an idiot I am.

"She's right," Peter says softly. "They're going to find out eventually."

"If they don't already know," Lynn adds.

I shoot her a look and she raises her hands in surrender.

"Look," she begins with a calm voice, "if this company is coming like Peter says they are, then all they have to do is watch the local station once. They'll find *you*." She stands, heading toward the door. "If I was some super-smart scientist and I came across a story of a random superperson showing up in the same town I sent my samples to..." she shrugs. "I'd be a little bit suspicious. Wouldn't you?"

Pursing my lips to the side, I stare at her. "Perhaps." I don't want to admit she's right.

"I have to run by the bank, but we aren't done with this conversation." She wiggles her finger at me and then Peter. "You two need to figure this shit out. You have superpowers," she juts her finger at me. "And you're a frickin' scientists." Her finger jabs toward Peter. "You don't need me to put the pieces together for you."

I gape at her because she's not wrong.

"Thank you for the coffee. I'll text you." Lynn winks then closes the door behind her.

"Well..." Peter begins, shoving his hands in his pocket.

I stand and join Peter as he strides into the office. We each take a seat and sit in thoughtful silence for a second before I speak up. "She's right. You should just tell them."

Peter signs, slumping in his seat. "Noah said the same thing."

"He did?"

Peter nods. "He was in my office when the email came through." He takes off his glasses and rubs his eyes. "Fine. I'll do it, but I need time to formulate all of this into words." He gestures at the stack of papers on the desk and then me. Leaning forward with a huff, he rests his elbows on the desk. "What would you say?"

"Looking forward to your visit. By the way my wife drank your compound. Sincerely, Peter McKenna," I tease.

"Where's Max when you need him? I bet he'd have an appropriate answer."

I feign a gasp and we both chuckle. "He would tell you to just tell the truth, because that's what *we* taught them. Coming clean always comes with a less heinous consequence than lying and being found out later."

CHAPTER 17

Two nights have passed without much action and no word from MSAD since Peter sent his email about the incident. No news is usually good news, but not in this case. The representatives from the company will arrive in a few days and we have no idea what to expect. Peter is nervous—rightfully so—and I'm doing my best to keep his mind elsewhere. So far, I kept to the shadows for a jewelry store break in. I didn't intervene, but I was itching to jump in and help the officers. Another night I witnessed a jay-walker almost become a hit-and-run while getting my hot dog and was able to yell at the man to jump back before the car careened into him. Reading minds has definitely come in handy lately.

I'm itching for something bigger though. With the impending unknown of what the MSAD people will do to me when they arrive, I want to use my abilities as much as possible for good.

Sitting in the car, I'm tapping my finger against the steering wheel listening to the scanner. As I lick a drop of ketchup from my thumb, finishing the snack, the scanner chirps with a 10-53.

"Car accident," I read from my list and shift the van into drive. I race to the scene knowing that the nearest EMT was ten minutes out. But in this lot, I'm only three minutes away. It's at an intersection I'm familiar with, one that has had accidents before because the stop signs are so far off the road they're barely noticeable. I don't know what I'll do to help yet, but if I can, I will.

I park under the cover of a large pine tree and jog to the accident at the end of the road. Two cars crashed into a T shape. Smoke billows from the one that raced from the left, and the one appearing as though it were going straight is bent along the driver's side.

Glass sprinkles the asphalt like glitter under the flickering street light and the smell of burnt rubber makes the air hot and putrid. I approach the collision, peeking through the windows to see if someone's still trapped inside. The car hit on the driver's side has two people in it. The person in the back looks young, and I rip the door open without a second thought. It's a boy, roughly ten years old. He looks up at the noise, blinking at me in confusion.

"It's okay. I'm here to help you," I say calmly. "Does anything hurt?"

He shakes his head, rubbing his chest where the seat belt sits tightly. His big brown eyes flicker to the front seat. "My m-mom?"

I follow his gaze, seeing a woman slumped over the steering wheel.

"I'm going to try and help both of you, okay?" I assure him. He's taking deep, jagged breaths, tugging at the belt. Reaching in, I jerk it once and it snaps free. "Try to catch your breath. Everything is going to be okay." His body begins to tremble as the shock settles on him. "What's your name?"

"B-Ben."

"Hi, Ben. My name is P.S. Jane," I say in the most soothing voice I can muster. He looks at me with wide-eyes. "That's right. Look at me. Can you breathe in slowly? Like this." I take a long inhale. Ben nods, mirroring my breath. "Good. That's great. Now let it out slowly through your mouth, okay?" I part my lips and release the air. Ben does the same. "That's perfect, Ben. Keep doing that while I check on your mom okay?"

Ben's eyes flutter, but he nods and I race from his door to the passenger door to assess the mom's situation. An airbag deployed, but is now deflated. She isn't moving, and I notice blood dripping onto the wheel, but I can see her chest ruse and she takes a breath.

I want to help get her out, but there's no way to tell what kind of damage her body has sustained from the impact. The driver side door is bent in at a horrid angle and the scent of blood is cloying as I lean into the window to get a better look. Her dark skin is ashen and there's a crimson stain on her shirt.

With a calming breath, I return to Ben. "You doing okay?" His head bobs once. "Good. Keep breathing like I showed you. I'm going to check on the other driver, okay?" He doesn't move, but I pause, watching as he takes another long inhale then let it out slowly. The trembling in his limbs as slowed, and now his chin is the only thing that quivers.

I race to the other car. The driver is male, and doesn't appear to be in good shape. The windshield is shattered as well as the window behind him. There's blood splattered across the dash. I stare at his chest looking for any sign of movement, but I can't tell if he's breathing or not. I focus my mind on him, hoping to hear his thoughts, but I'm only met with silence.

Sirens sound in the distance growing closer. I silently thank whatever being is out there watching over us that help is here.

With a gulp, I step back and examine the cars. The scent of gasoline greets me as I inhale, overpowering the aroma of burnt rubber. I've seen a lot of car accidents in movies, and this is often the point where the characters dash away before the vehicles erupt into a fiery explosion.

Panicked thoughts from Ben jolt into my mind. He's terrified, and I can't blame him.

I go back to him, crouching to his level.

"Hey, Ben." He stares at me, and I can see the panic in them. "I need you to be brave, okay? The ambulance is almost here and we will get you and your mom out."

"I-I'm scared," he whispers, wiping tears from his cheek.

"I know you are, and I am, too." I glance out the front window. Red and blue lights are coming. "I'm going to check on your mom real quick."

"Okay."

I squeeze his shoulders once, then yank on the passenger door. It creaks open and I slip onto the seat.

What's happening... I hear a faint thought and detect the woman raising her head. She's blinking through the window and panic strikes her and she turns to look in the back seat. *Ben. Where is Ben?!*

"Mommy!" Ben cries from the back seat.

"Ben? Ben, are you okay?"

"He's doing fine," I tell her. She swings her gaze to me and winces. "Hi. Please try not to move too much. The ambulance is almost here."

"W-who are you?" Her eyes flutter as if she's about to pass out. From the amount of blood dripping from her exposed temple, I can only imagine how dizzy she is.

I give her a warm smile. "I'm P.S. Jane." Her eyes narrow, trailing over the top half of my suit.

She lifts her head and I see her trying to move her arm. The woman sucks in a sharp breath. "My arm. It-it really hurts." Tears fill her eyes.

"Alright, try not to move too much. Does anything else hurt?"

Her head sways. "I-I'm not s-sure," she stammers, almost breathlessly. "Ben? Honey?"

"Mommy, I'm scared," he sniffs.

She nods, laying her head against the headrest. "I know baby, but we're going to be just fine."

"You will be," I say. "Both of you." I glance at Ben. "I'm going to see if I can get to your door. The faster the paramedics can get you out the better, right?" I don't wait for her to reply as I slip out of the seat. Glass cracks under every step as I round to the impact point. The air is thick with smoke and gas; a cloying combination that makes me cough and gag.

Finding where the two cars are connected, I reach down and do my best to grab whatever part of the male driver's car I can. If I can get a good enough grip, I should be able to pry it backwards and get to her door.

There's no way to do this gracefully, so I take a deep breath, and pull... and pull... until one car begins to groan. Heat rises from the car I'm bent over, hitting me in the face. Sweat beads on my brow.

When I run out of air, I pause, drawing my hands away and shaking them out. Bits of my gloves are torn, and the tips of my fingers feel burned, but I can't stop. I wipe my brow and grip the car again. As I grit my teeth to pull, the sound of sirens and clashing thoughts hit my mind. The darkness fills with flashing lights. Doors slam and footsteps pound toward me.

Shit. I think, but I can't flee. Not yet. I can get these cars apart faster than they can get their tools to do it. Instead, I wave my hands over my head and shout, "Over here! I need help!"

Two firefighters approach me, halting as they realize they're standing in front of a woman in a super suit.

"You're—" One man begins.

"Yes, I'm P.S. Jane. Thanks for noticing. Look, there's a boy in the back, the mom is in and out of consciousness," I explain. "The driver of this car," I say, pointing to the still unconscious driver, "is unresponsive so far. As soon as I disconnect the two cars, you can get them out, right? So let's go."

"You need to get out of the way, ma'am and let us do our job," the tallest one says to me.

I groan in frustration. "Look, I'm strong, like *really* strong, and I can help move the cars apart before you can get your device out and ready to go."

The two firefighters exchange curious glances.

"I won't get in your way. I'll help you move the cars apart and step back, I swear." I hold up my hand in promise.

"Come on then. We're wasting time," the female one says. She turns to the EMTs and shouts something at them. I don't listen, and do my best to tune out their thoughts so I can focus my energy on the cars again.

Wrapping my fingers around whatever scalding part I'm able to grip, I force myself to forget about the pain in my hand, clench my jaw, and pull as hard as I can. This time, I can feel the cars separate. A loud screech draws silence around me. I can feel the eyes of everyone on the back of my neck and it's as hot as the steam, or whatever it is, rising from the car under my nose.

There's a few inches of space between the two cars now, and gloved hands grip the opposite side, pairs and pairs of them, helping me draw the cars apart. As soon as there's enough space, one firefighter steps in and tries to pry the door off.

"It's stuck," he says, gesturing to someone in the distance.

"Let me try." I shift to grab the warped door frame and tug. It inches away with a creak. Rolling my shoulders, I plant my feet and heave back. The door breaks free, clattering to the ground. Two firefighters jump in to get the woman out, and others have moved to assess the male driver. Ben is already out of the car standing on the side of the road with a paramedic. Those who are waiting for instructions, or for the people to be free, are clapping.

I turn in a daze at the surrounding group. EMTs, firefighters, police… a large group of them are surrounding the collision observing me.

One officer approaches, and I recognize him.

"Officer Richards." I sigh, feeling out of breath, but I smile at him.

"P.S. Jane," he says with a shake of his head. "I didn't think I'd see you again with how our last visit ended… when you said it was a one time thing."

I shrug. "I was close by."

Officer Richards lets out a sharp exhale. "You're going to cause a lot of trouble showing up uninvited."

"Maybe someone should invite me then." I tip my head at him and raise my brows. He stares at me with a look of frustration on his face. "Are you going to arrest me?"

His almond eyes flicker behind me. "The Chief was pretty upset with me after he heard I let you go the other night."

"We got them out safely, didn't we?" I put my hands on my hips, turning to watch the paramedics ease the unconscious man from his vehicle. "That's what matters."

Handcuffs jingle at my side. "I don't want to bring you in in cuffs," he says as I face him once more. "But the Chief does have questions for you… demands."

"What kind of demands?"

"One is to stop. Mind your own business. He thinks you're a menace. Out for attention. Some bored, possibly unstable, woman looking for a thrill or something." A quiet smile tugs at the corner of his lips.

I watch him. "And what do you think?"

Officer Richards considers his words as one ambulance drives off, siren blaring. "I think I saw you lift a pole out of the ground in a single tug and tear two cars apart with your bare hands."

"I did have help."

He scoffs with a smile. "Yeah, but what you did on your own was impressive." Twirling the cuffs on his finger, he continues. "I believe you have some sort of super thing going on. I believe you really are wanting to just help and do good."

"But..."

"But," he says, tucking the cuffs back into his belt. "Others are less convinced."

A tow truck arrives, backing in to remove the cars. We step aside to make room and watch as they load the woman's car onto the ramp. With a quick glance, I realize I can slip away without being noticed. Not by anyone but Officer Richards, at least. I hesitate, but then step back.

"Where are you going?"

I gesture to the scene. "You all have this under control. I know when my job is done."

He nods once, then glances between me and the accident. "Thank you for your help tonight."

"Anytime," I say, backing away, but his thoughts stop me.

We should get that woman a bat signal or something.

"I think my son would think that is a great idea, too." I curl my lips into a mischievous smile that only confuses the officer. With a wink, I tap my head and take another step away. "I'm always listening. One way or another. I'll know when to find *you*." And with that, I turn and press through the line of trees, keeping to the shadows back to my waiting van.

CHAPTER 18

Over the past few days, I've been exchanging texts with Rebecca. She wanted to collaborate on our ideas to see how well we could work together if they vote me on as vice president. Naturally, I was eager to share my thoughts about the upcoming fundraisers, and Rebecca took all my ideas with a graceful stride. Shockingly, the haughty demeanor she's always had toward me has defrosted and her friendly nature has sprouted. Odd, but I think we're kind of friends now.

"I'd still be cautious of that bitch," Lynn advises me, perched on the edge of my couch.

"I think she's coming around to the idea of having some extra help with running the PTA. I sense there's something more going on we don't know about. She seems…"

"Possessed?"

I roll my eyes. "Overwhelmed. Distracted." I shrug, unwrapping the bandages on my hand. The burns look better, but I'm missing the PTA meeting this afternoon as I don't want everyone to question why I'm suddenly wearing driving gloves inside, or why my hands look like I stuck them in a blender. They're healing, but they're still ugly.

Lynn winces as she watches me. "Are you sure you don't want to come to the meeting? I'm sure half of them suspect you're the new super in town. Might as well show yourself off."

I shake my head. "There are too many questions I'm not ready to answer yet, but I will be at the next meeting. Swear it."

"You are all over the news." Lynn sips her iced coffee.

I sigh, leaning against the cushions. "Not me. P.S. Jane."

"Same. Thing," Lynn enunciates. "You do realize you're the biggest thing that's happened in Brightwood in probably decades. It's amazing what you can do and that you actually want to use it for something positive. Give yourself some credit."

"Thanks." I lift the ice coffee she brought me and take a long drink. The coldness of the cup feels wonderful against my fingers. I may have special abilities, but quick healing is not one of them.

"One of these nights you're going to let me help, right? Be the girl in the chair or eyes in the sky or whatever." She flutters her free hand about.

I laugh. "Eye in the sky? We don't have that kind of funding, Lynn," I tease. "But, yes. Peter is exhausted and juggling a lot. He could use the help. He slept through the entire event the other night. Not a single word on the comms during the entire incident!"

"I would have loved to been on the other end of that Bluetooth. Listening in. Giving advice. Googling... things." Standing, she grabs her purse. "You let me know when it's my turn, but I should head to the meeting. I'd hate to be late and have your new best friend bear her claws at me." We share a chuckle. "I'll text you what you miss, okay?"

"Thank you." I wave as she leaves.

A few hours later, my phone rings. It's Lynn and I eagerly answer. "Hey, how'd the meeting go?"

"I told you not to trust that bitch," Lynn spits, and I can hear her frustration in her tone.

"What happened?"

Lynn scoffs. "Hold on, I'm sending you a photo."

I turn the speakerphone on and wait for the text to come through. When it does, my jaw drops.

"That bitch!"

Lynn sighs. "I warned you."

The photo Lynn sent is of the giant notebook Rebecca uses to jot ideas down. Normally, the scribbled key points are messy as Suzy hastily writes, but these are organized, precise. They're Rebecca's perfect handwriting and something she'd prepared before the meeting.

"She's claiming they're *her* ideas," Lynn explains. "Everyone thinks she's had this huge epiphany or enlightenment or whatever. You know she's never had great ideas to begin with, and suddenly, boom, she has this grand list."

"Those are *my* ideas!" I shout. "Rebecca and I were discussing them just the other day. How could she—" but suddenly, it all makes sense. Rebecca befriending me, wanting to meet and chat about upcoming events, wanting to hear my ideas so we could correlate our notes. That wicked woman was stealing my plans and using them as her own to make herself look like frickin' gold! I should have seen it coming. Hell, it's Rebecca! Everyone knows she's a wicked witch. For some reason, I let the fact that, perhaps, she did want to be friends, that she *was* interested in my ideas, cloud my judgment. Or perhaps, being a super has my head all messed up and I can't determine the difference between fake bitches and real friends anymore. Maybe I'm becoming too trusting and friendly... time to rein that shit in.

Lynn huffs into the phone. "I know. I recognized a few of them right away, because you've mentioned them to me, but of course when I tried to claim them for you, she brushed it off saying I must have heard it from you when *she* told *you* about it over coffee last week."

"That bitch!" I bite the words, gripping my phone so tight that it makes a threatening cracking sound. With a slow exhale, I calm my temper and loosen my grip. "When's the next meeting?"

"Tuesday."

That meant I had five days to come up with a plan to take her down.

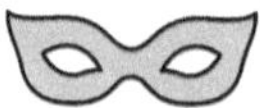

My mind is spinning with ideas to show Rebecca I mean business. What kind of business? PTA business, of course. Something I never thought I'd be so passionate about. But knowing she's stolen my ideas as her own, and the other PTA members probably think she's some amazing genius now, makes something boil within me. Rage. Annoyance. Frustration. It's all there, bubbling, waiting to overflow like a pot on the stove.

I'm not even paying attention to the police scanner tonight. I'm hyper focused on Rebecca. So focused, I ate *two* hot dogs to fuel the heat inside me. Thankfully, there's nothing happening tonight, and the scanner remains quiet.

It's still early, so I take my phone and stab at the keyboard.

(Me) I know you used my ideas at the meeting.

(Rebecca) I'm not sure I know what you mean, Jane.

(Me) Don't be daft. Lynn showed me a photo of the notes.

(Rebecca) Maybe if you had been there, this wouldn't have happened.

(Me) Would it really have mattered?

(Rebecca) When we discussed ideas together, it became an agreement that they were our

ideas. Not just yours, Jane. Plus, you can't claim free-thought. Our conversations inspired me!

(Me) Inspired you to write the same ideas I had? Spring Talent Show. Neighborhood Clean Up. Plant a Tree... those were my words EXACTLY.

I'm fuming. Puffing breath through my nose like a dragon building fire inside. But this bitch thinks she can steal my ideas. My gold! Claiming it as her own hoard. Rebecca has another thing coming to her.

(Rebecca) Perhaps if you cared enough, you would have shown up to the meeting. It's not on me that you don't take PTA as seriously as I do. It's not a great look for a possible vice president.

(Me) I think I'd rather run the show myself.

(Rebecca) You wouldn't dare.

(Me) Watch me, Rebecca. You brought this upon yourself.

(Rebecca) No one will believe you actually want to take that responsibility. You're a joke, Jane. You've never been serious about PTA events. Everyone knows you're just there because you're a bored housewife who has nothing better to do. You can't even sell silicone to soccer moms anymore. You have nothing. If you're bored, perhaps you should take up a hobby like knitting. But don't come after something people actually need to care about. That's pathetic and selfish.

My jaw drops and my fingers grip my phone. A small crack spreads across the screen, but I can't stop the rage running through my veins like lava. Clenching my jaw, I type one last reply.

(Me) The PTA sees right through your little act, Rebecca. We all know you're just running the PTA because you, too, have nothing better to do. You're vile. Wicked. And none of us like you. I can see why your husband disappears for weeks at a time on those 'business trips.' I'm sure he enjoys the silence from your constant nagging. I'm doing everyone a favor by wanting to be president. You can't stop me.

(Rebecca) You think you suddenly run this place, but I know your secret, Jane. I know who you really are. If you keep pushing to take my place, I'll let everyone know what you're really up to.

Does she know I'm P.S. Jane? Lynn said it would be easy for anyone who knows me to see the super is clearly *me*. But Rebecca? There's no way she's watching local news. Someone like her, posh and nose in the air, only watches world news I bet.

I stare out the front window, considering how to best respond, but a threat like that isn't something I can type a middle finger emoji to and hope it ends well. Instead, I set my phone in the passenger seat and lean my head against the steering wheel.

"What are you doing, Jane?" I chide to myself.

The scanner hums. Dispatch comes across in a serious tone that sends a chill down my spine.

"Attention all available officers. We have a 10-34 at Hotel Libra. All officers proceed to the call. Wait for further instructions."

A bomb threat? The adrenaline is exactly what I need to clear my mind. I crank the van on and hit the button on the bluetooth.

"Peter? I'm headed to the Hotel Libra."

Yawning, he replies, "What's going on?"

"Bomb threat."

"Jane." His voice is clear, the mere words bringing him to life. "You should let the professionals handle this."

Shaking my head, I back out of my parking space. "I'm not going to run into the building. I'll just park as close as I can and observe." My blinker signals left and I head toward the Hotel. It's only a few blocks away, and there's a parking garage where I can leave the van in a few buildings down. "I'll check in if anything changes."

"Copy that. Be careful."

"I will," I tell him, then disconnect the call. We both agreed it was best for me to call only when I need him, or to update him on the situation. Since he fell asleep during the last event, I've felt bad. Peter still needs sleep, unlike me, and staying up a few times a week to sit and wait for me to fight crime wasn't fair to him. So, instead, he naps, waiting for any news I have for him.

After parking in the garage, I wait, listening to the scanner for any updates. I promised I wouldn't run in without information, or put myself in harm's way. So I sit, heart racing, drumming my fingers on the steering wheel.

"Officer Landon, on the scene," a rough, male voice comes through the scanner.

"Copy. Bomb crew three minutes out."

"Officer Baker, on scene," a female officer chirps along with two others.

There isn't a lot of dialogue exchange on the situation, and my legs are itching to get out and stretch. Cautiously, I leave the van and head around the corner to the scene.

They blocked the road with police cars. Officers are posted at different areas, some by the cars, some grouped in deep discussion, and others waiting for orders off to the side. I hang back in the shadow near the alley, trying to focus my attention on the thoughts of the group nearest me.

No contact yet. Probably just a romantic quarrel.

I hope everyone is okay inside.

How many hostages did they say?

And then there are too many voices screaming in my head and I have to force them out. I'm dizzy, and I take a second to balance myself before walking straight up to the nearest officer.

"Excuse me," I say. He turns, and his eyes go wide. "Hi, there. I'm wondering if I can be of any assistance."

His gaze sweeps over me, and he scoffs. "I don't think so. Chief warned us you may show up." He rolls his pale blue eyes at me. *Great. Just what we need. The crazy superwoman.* "My orders are to tell you to not interfere. Go home, *P.S. Jane.*" The tone is mocking and he turns from me as if our conversation is over with. The hell it is.

I feel the stares of the crowd on me. Whispers make their way to me, but I don't need them to hear what they're thinking. Some believe in my cause, cheering that I've arrived. Internally, I smile because Max would be so happy by their thoughts. Others are cursing me, scoffing at the idea of someone like me thinking I could be of any use. I throw a glare over my shoulder at a particular thought that crosses my mind. A man notices my attention on him and lifts his chin. Raising his right hand, he flips me the bird. Lovely.

With a sigh, I push the thoughts from my mind and call to the officer who is now walking away from me. "Have you made contact with the one who claims there's a bomb?"

He pauses, turning halfway to look at me. "I can't talk to you about the situation, ma'am. Please stay back and let us do our job."

I wrinkle my nose in frustration. Glancing at the other officers, I search for a familiar face. I follow the police tape, rounding the scene until another officer catches my attention. Office Richards gives me a small wave. It's enough of a gesture for those nearest him to look in my direction.

"Her again?" one of the female officers remarks. I roll my eyes, placing my hands on my hips.

Office Richards says something to the group then walks toward me. "P.S. Jane. We were all wondering if you'd show up tonight." He smiles, but it's almost apologetic.

"I heard about the threat," I say, lowering my voice. "I know I'm no expert, but I do have some skills that may be handy in this situation."

His eyebrow lifts. "I don't think this is the appropriate time for you to step in."

"I can't stop a bomb or go invisible to get inside, but maybe I can help in another way." I flash him my best hero smile, lifting my chin slightly in confidence. This is exactly what I need to get my mind off Rebecca and use the pent up energy I have. Better to use it for good than showing up at her door for a slap in the face.

Officer Richards shakes his head. "I'm sorry. I can't let you cross the police line."

My smile drops. "Okay. Fine." I bounce on my feet wanting to argue. To tell him that I am helpful and I can be a team player if they'd only let me. I'm not just some civilian wanting to the star hero, I'm an actual hero just looking to help!

Someone calls for Office Richards and he shoots me a friendly grin before heading back to his team.

Chewing on my bottom lip, I ease around the perimeter some more until I'm closer to a gathered group of officers. They're speaking softly to each other, but I tune into their thoughts to see what's going on. An older gentleman with gray hair and an authoritative voice enters my mind.

No contact. No sign of threat. No demands. Probably a hoax, but I'd rather not take that chance.

I purse my lips to the side, listening to each officers internal debate on the situation. Some want to storm the building, bust down doors, and demand the threatener release the hostages. They believe the threat is fake, but others are more hesitant to jump, wanting to take their time, try to make contact and work out a deal with whoever is holding people inside.

We don't even know where they are in the building. There's no way to contact them.

"Excuse me!" I call to them. All eyes land on me. "How do you plan to move forward is you can't even make contact?" The older gentleman I assume is in charge narrows his gaze at me. "Sorry to interrupt, but if the *accused*," I say instead of bomber not wanting to cause any more panic around me then there already is, "hasn't made contact with you all yet, and you have no way to know where he is exactly, how do you plan to proceed?"

The man scratches his jaw and sniffs. "You must be P.S. Jane." He steps toward me, and I take a peek at the tag on his vest reading Brown. Shit. I've just placed myself directly in front of the man who has been wanting me to hop a ticket to the nearest station and turn myself in.

"I am," I say with as much confidence as I can.

He inches closer and lowers his voice. "I thought we made it very clear that we do *not* want you to interfere with official police business."

"So I've heard."

"Then why are you here?" he seethes, hawk eyes holding mine.

"I believe I can help you, sir."

His fuzzy brows draw together and his eyes dance over my entire body. It sends a shudder down my spine and takes everything in me to not show that I'm slightly intimidated by him.

Chief Brown scoffs. "I don't have time for this. For *you*. We have a serious situation on our hands and the last thing I need is for some wack job civilian to play hero. I suggest you take my advice and hang up that ridiculous costume of yours and go back to dusting and hosting dinner parties."

I watch as he returns to the group, too stunned to respond. Officer Richards glances in my direction but doesn't dare make a gesture toward me. I don't take the Chief's advice, instead I stand there, watching, listening, and waiting for the right time to jump in because I will prove how useful I can be, one way or another.

"Send in a team to sweep every floor. As far as we know, the call came from the fourth floor, but he could have moved the hostages. If they continue to refuse contact, we will take each room by force."

The team around him moves, forming groups and shouting orders at each other. Soon, a team of four is headed to the front door.

"What about hostages?" I ask, watching the group step into formation.

The commander huffs, turning to me with a glare. "I didn't say anything about hostages."

"That one did." I point to the voice I heard earlier, trying to recall the details of the case. "Well, he didn't *say* anything about them, but I heard him trying to remember how many there were inside."

He tilts his head slightly. "You heard?"

I nod. "I also know you believe this could be a hoax, but you're not willing to take the chance."

His nose flares. "I didn't—"

"You don't have to. I can read minds, sir."

"I don't care if you can see through walls or fart rainbows out your ass," the chief snaps, stalking toward me. His ebony boots thunk against the concrete in a threatening rhythm. "You may think you're something special out there," he thrusts his chin in the direction of the rural neighborhoods. "But in here, you're just another civilian getting in my way."

"But, Chief—"

"Officer Larken, please escort P.S. Jane to your vehicle," he says to a female officer. She nods, striding her petite figure toward me. I notice one hand reaching for her cuffs.

I always get stuck babysitting. Officer Larken thinks with a grimace.

I slip my finger over my ear, as if tucking a loose strand of hair, and press the tiny Bluetooth on. It's small, and can only be seen if one knows to look for it or is staring directly at my profile. A chime lets me know Peter has picked up.

"Yello," he says cheerfully. Too cheerfully for the situation before me.

I watch Larken approach, ducking under the police tape.

"Jane?" Peter's voice becomes thick with worry. "Are you there?"

As the officer grips my forearm with her long fingers, I wince.

"What are you going to do? Arrest me?" I ask her as she leads me back under the tape and toward a waiting police car.

She scoffs. "Not unless I have to."

"Jane, are-are you getting arrested?" Peter almost shouts. "Fuck." A loud thud strikes my ears.

"There are *hostages* in there," I begin, almost pleading for her to hear me and let me go. "People who are trapped. Without any help. And some psycho who is going to blow them up at a drop of a hat!"

Officer Larken whips me to face her. "I know what a hostage is." Her eyes narrow. "And you're one to talk about a psycho jumping into action in a split second. Do you even hear yourself? You sound insane!" Her voice rises as she resumes walking, picking up her pace.

"What the hell is going on?" Peter asks loudly.

"Listen," I say to not just the officer, but to Peter as well. "I can help. I know I can." Jerking my arm from her grip I stare at her deep brown eyes. "I know you think you're stuck babysitting the crazy woman, but the last thing I want is for anyone to get hurt. If I can get in there, I can hear exactly where everyone is. Without barreling through every single door and startling him to literal death."

"Jane, stop! You do not need to go into a bomb situation," Peter chimes in.

Officer Larken's brows draw together and her gaze flickers over my shoulder. "I'm just following orders." Her voice softens as if maybe—just maybe—she believes me.

I perk at her tone and begin to step away. Her hand is around my arm again so fast, my foot isn't even back on the ground.

"I don't think so, lady."

"But—"

She yanks me within inches of her face. "I will put you in cuffs and lock you in this car if you can't come quietly. Understood?"

I am so tired of people thinking I've lost my mind. Tired of this community not believing in me. I will prove my worth to them. The chief will see how valuable I can be.

"Peter," I say, staring directly into the officer's eyes. Her features shift from annoyance to confusion. "I'm going inside."

"Jane, no. Please. Let them handle it."

"I'll be safe."

Officer Larken is saying something, but I'm ignoring her, focusing on Peter's voice.

"Don't. Don't go in there."

"I have to do this. They're never going to let me help unless I prove that I'm an asset."

Peter sniffs. "Jane."

"I love you." And before he can respond, I reach up and remove the Bluetooth, handing it to the bewildered officer. "Hang on to this for me."

"What? No," she objects, but I don't give her a second to reach for her cuffs. Instead, I thrust the device into her hand and shove her shoulder so she spins away from me. With the momentum, the woman topples, falling to the concrete with an oomph as I run across the lot and through the front door of the hotel. Officers pursue me. I hear them shouting my name, but I don't stop.

I heard one of the officers mention the caller may be on the fourth floor, so I take the stairs—a huge mistake on my part—and huff my way up each flight. By the time I reach the exit to the fourth floor, I'm panting. Sweat drips down my brow and I wipe it away with my gloved hand.

"Okay, Jane. This is it. This is your moment."

I quiet my mind and focus on the silent hallway before me. Taking slow, soft steps, I pad down the ugly carpet glancing at each closed door. I'm only about ten feet from the stairway door when thoughts race through my mind. I can't tell how far away they are, but I know I'm close. Continuing forward, the panicked voices thunder in my mind. I do my best to filter through them, listening for one tone in particular.

I'll do it. Blow this shit hole up. Try to fire me. For what? Nothing! They'll pay.

With a tip of my head, as if tuning in to this particular voice, I hold my breath and take a few more steps. The thoughts grow louder, and soon, it's as if the person it comes from is standing right beside me. Taking a step closer to the door on my left, I listen. Then, I do the same on the right. A tingle runs over my body.

This is the room. This is where the hostages are. This is where the bomb is.

The elevator dings, signaling its arrival. I pivot toward the noise and find a team of officers spilling from its enclosure. With raised runs, they move down the hall, right to me.

My chest tightens. All the air in my lungs expels itself in one sharp exhale. The officer in the front of the pack signals, and the others swarm around him. Their steps are silent, but I know if the bomber is close enough to the door, he'll see the shadows pass by.

I wave my hands at them, motioning for them to shush. Using overexaggerated hand gestures, I try to convey that the room beside me is the one they need. The officer in the lead tips his head. He's wearing a helmet, but even so, I can tell his brows have furrowed.

The female officer from before creeps forward, withdrawing her cuffs as quietly as she can. I shake my head, lifting my hands in surrender and stepping toward her instead. My job here is done. I found the room without causing anyone to get hurt.

As I approach the woman, her seething frown greets me. I hold out my wrists for her and she slips the cuffs around them, snapping them so tightly I wince.

"No funny business," she whispers, gripping my arm with one hand and shoving me toward the elevator. It's only a few doors away, so it takes us seconds to get there. She jabs her finger at the down button and huffs. "You may have helped find the room, but that doesn't mean you're off the hook."

As the elevator chimes and the doors part, I take a final glance over my shoulder. The group is prepared to break down the door, pressed along the wall, ready to rush the room. I watch as one officer lifts what appears to be a type of battering ram and position himself.

"He should have just asked for a keycard," I start, and the female officer with the vice on my arm scoffs. "Or I could just kick it down for them."

She jerks me in the direction of the elevator once, but I stand firm. "They have this handled." Her voice is thick with annoyance. I side-eye her as she moves beside me.

I'm about to shove this woman into the god damn—

I roll my eyes and shut out her thoughts. "No. Seriously. I'm really strong—"

Before I can finish my explanation, the battering ram connects with the door. A loud crack echoes down the silent hall, and then, in a whoosh, a blast of heat hits me, shoving me off my feet and forcing me to the ground.

CHAPTER 19

Smoke fills my lungs, burning and scratching at my throat. My entire body feels like it's on fire and there's something heavy on my legs. I press my elbows into the hotel carpet and lift myself enough to see what happened. The officer escorting me is on my lower half, rolling off me slowly and easing to their feet. She reaches for me, but I decline her offer, getting up unsteadily.

"We have to get to the stairs," she tells me, then coughs, but I don't respond because I'm staring at the fire blazing behind us. The officer is talking into her radio, but the words mangle in my mind as the thoughts of everyone entering the building hits me.

Dizziness washes over me. With every blink, the scene before me becomes hazy and filled with stars. Someone, the officer, I assume, grabs my arm, yanking me down the hall toward the stairs. Firefighters and other workers pass us in the stairwell, heading toward where the bomb went off. When my feet hit the pavement, I stumble.

The voices are too much. Too many people are screaming and their panic overwhelms me. Stars fill the edges of my eyes at the noise. I can't focus on any one voice. They're jumbled together as if I'm standing in the middle of a crowded arena, everyone shouting at whoever is performing on stage. Except instead of praise and cheers, they're screams of pain and terror.

Hands lift me to my feet, and I blink at the EMT trying to help me to a nearby ambulance. He's shouting, but I can't hear him over the buzzing in my mind. The voices are a deafening garble. I swing my attention over my shoulder, where smoke is billowing from the fourth floor. There's a gaping hole where the windows once sat and cracks expelling from the damage.

Tears flood my vision, and I gasp. Darkness edges in and I'm helped into the ambulance. As the doors close, I collapse against the gurney.

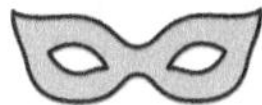

Pain radiates over my entire body. Fluttering my eyes open, there's brightness all around me. Images of the smoke and dread from the scene come back to me. Breathing heavily, I clench my fingers around the sheets. They're cold and scratchy. I shut my eyes to the noise around me and inside my mind. It's loud and grating against my skull. *Hush.* I think, shushing the voices into silence.

"Hey, Jane. You're okay." Peter's voice comes through the chaos in my mind, calming them like a cool breeze. His hand encloses around mine, and I grab at him like life support. "She's awake," he calls.

"Jane? Jane, can you open your eyes?" A female voice I don't recognize comes near.

My eyes are heavy and feel like they're glued shut, but I crack them open again. Bit by bit, the hospital room comes into focus. Beeping machines trill nearby and tubes extend from my arm.

"There you are," the female voice says cheerfully. I glance at her, a tall, slender woman with rich brown hair and kind green eyes. "I'm Doctor Shields. How are you feeling?" She peers at the monitor, then stares at me.

"Fantastic," I grouse, my voice raspy. Peter hands me a cup of water and I take it thankfully, downing it in a few gulps. It stings against my throat, but already it feels better.

"Your throat is going to be sore for a while, but no lasting damage from the smoke," the doctor explains. "How's your pain level?"

I press onto my elbows, scooting into a more comfortable position. The movement makes me wince as pain sparks down my back. "Uh, seven?" I say, unsure what to compare it to.

The doctor nods, adjusts a few settings on the monitor, then smiles at me. "I'll let you rest, but a nurse will be in soon to take your vitals." She pats my shoulder before leaving.

Pain meds settle into my system, making my eyes droop, but I blink and turn to Peter. He's watching me with a worried gaze. With a sigh, he leans his elbows on his knees.

"Jane, what the hell happened?" Peter's voice is whisper soft.

I lick my chapped lips before answering him. "I wasn't going to go inside," I began. "But... but I knew I could help them, if they'd just let me."

"That wasn't your responsibility. The police have specialized teams for these kinds of things."

"I know, but—"

"But what, Jane?" he interrupts harshly. His brows are drawn together in a fierce display of disappointment. "You're not a police officer or a firefighter or any part of those teams. You're just..." Peter stops with a huff, unable to say the words he knows will cut through me.

"Just what? Just a woman? Just another civilian? Just another deranged lady looking for attention?" I scoff, adjusting the tubes so I don't tug them out as I shift. "I thought you were on my side."

Peter exhales sharply, slumping into his chair. "I am. You know I'm on your side. But this whole running into a building with a *bomb* thing was not part of our plan. And if I recall, it was the one thing you said you *wouldn't* be doing. You're not invincible, Jane. You could have died in that explosion."

I stare at him. "They had *hostages*, Peter. I couldn't just let the officers run in blind. If they gave away their position too early, they could have set the bomb off. When I heard they were going to do exactly that..." I huff, shaking my head. "I told them I could read minds, that I would help them locate the room they were being held in, but they refused my help."

"No shit they refused." Peter's voice rises. "You may have super abilities, but this is real life. *Your life.* And you just ran into the epicenter of disaster!"

"I got in just fine, thank you. And I did locate the perpetrator. And an officer escorted me out." I fail to mention that it was a forced evacuation, but I can tell from his thoughts he knows that's exactly what I meant.

"*Out?*" Peter's tone hardens. "Jane, you got blasted into the elevator doors. Even with your help, the bomb *still* went off. The hostages all died!" He takes a calming breath because his voice is rising.

Died. Every single one of them. His thoughts sound in my mind. I'm taken aback by his harshness, but he's right. Even after everything I tried to do, it was for nothing. I avert my gaze, unable to look Peter in the eyes as my own mist.

"You were foolish to think this through on your own. If you had told me... why didn't you contact me?" Scooting to the edge of his chair, he reaches for my hand, taking it gently.

Tears blur my vision, and like a winter blanket, listlessness falls over me. "I couldn't... there wasn't... time," I manage through deep inhales.

Sleep is overcoming me and there's nothing I can do about it.

"There's always time," Peter says, and then my eyes are drifting shut and I'm unable to open them again.

Among the darkness, images of burning buildings flicker to life. I can almost feel the flames against my skin, hear the screams of those left behind, smell the smoke... and then I'm gasping awake as a hand touches my wrist.

"Sorry," a nurse whispers, shooting me an apologetic smile. "Just checking your vitals." He jots down a few notes on a clipboard and examines the beeping machines.

Glancing around, the room is empty.

"My husband?" I ask, voice still groggy.

"He stepped out about an hour ago, but he said he'd be back later this morning."

I nod, turning to see the faint light streaming in from the blinds over the window.

"You're all over the news," the nurse remarks. When I turn to him, he has a sly smile on his face, and I furrow my brows at him in confusion. "You're P.S. Jane, right? The super." His eyes widen, sparkling with secrets.

I don't confirm, but it doesn't seem I need to because he keeps on about the story, the bomb, the super—*me*—that was there.

"Can you really read minds?"

I clear my throat and nod. He squints, and I can tell he's trying to get me to read his thoughts. I tune into them for a split second.

Banana cream pie.

"You're thinking about banana cream pie," I say, drawing the sheets higher. There's a chill in the room, and I want nothing more than for this nurse to leave.

He gawks with a chuckle. "Wow, that's right! Everyone on the floor is talking about you, but don't worry, we are making sure no one visits who isn't your immediate family. Fans have been trying to get into the building, though, claiming to be your second cousin or whatever." He chuckles. "Your husband left a list."

"Lynn. Can you make sure Lynn Cormack is on the list?"

"Of course. I'll go add the name now. Get some rest."

As soon as the door clicks shut, I'm fumbling for the remote, flipping through channels to find a news station.

"... Our very own local hero..." I pass the channel but quickly turn back.

The nurse was right... I'm all over the news. They must have taken clips from the hotel security cameras when we entered the building. I'm standing in the center of the hall flanked by officers, my bright suit against their dark armor inching across the lobby.

"After the explosion, P.S. Jane was taken directly to Memorial East, where she is getting treatment for first and second-degree burns along with Officer Lindsay Monroe," the female reporter claims. Then a family photo fills a tiny box in the screen's corner.

"An anonymous source claims that our superhero is rumored to be Jane McKenna, wife of Professor Peter McKenna, who teaches science at the university." The male reporter continues talking about my family, but I can't hear him anymore. The buzzing in my ears intensifies and my vision tunnels.

They know who I am. My heart rate increases, making the machine beeping beside me rise in tempo.

"Everyone is talking about poor Jane," a voice draws me from my daze and a shadow fills the entryway. I didn't hear the door open, but it shuts with a snap and the shadowy figure moves closer. With a small bouquet,

Rebecca enters the pool of light from the window. "Hello, Jane."

"Rebecca? What are you doing here?"

"When the PTA heard about your *accident,* we all pitched in on flowers," she replies, picking at a daisy in the bunch. With a jerk, the petal dislodges and Rebecca let it flutter to the floor.

"How did you get visitation? There's a list—"

Rebecca scoffs and flashes her pearly teeth. "I'm the president of the PTA, and well known here for my volunteer work. It wasn't hard to persuade them we were close friends." She saunters across the tile, setting the vase on the side table, and takes a seat. "Plus, your nurse is a close acquaintance. He allowed me in just this once."

I seethe at the closed door, hoping that the nurse feels my glare. *Ass.* So much for a fucking list of approved visitors.

The silence is awkward as Rebecca's dark eyes move over me. Her expression is unreadable and an uncomfortable unease settles on me. I focus my mind on her thoughts, hoping to understand why she is here.

Poor, pathetic Jane. Is all I hear before Rebecca clears her throat, narrowing her gaze.

"How about we stay out of each other's minds, shall we?" she sneers. I wonder how she knew I was listening. My face must have given away my question, because she chuckles. "You make this face when you're *reading minds.* If that's true at all." She rolls her eyes. "It's a tell I noticed a few meetings ago. I thought it was an odd tick, but now it all makes sense."

"Not like you have much worth listening to in there anyway," I disclose, and her smile falters. Shifting so I'm sitting straighter, I reach for the water cup.

"Let me," Rebecca offers, standing and filling the plastic cup. She doesn't hand it to me right away, but eases it toward me with pursed lips.

Taking the cup, I observe her. Something doesn't feel right about this situation. As I sip the water, it's warm and does nothing to quench my thirst.

"I assume this isn't just another social call. Us becoming friends being a scam to steal my ideas and all. So why are you really here, Rebecca?" I set the half-filled cup down and watch her. She moves back to the seat, sitting with a graceful ease, and folds her hands in her lap.

"People *love* the new super-Jane," she says with a groan of disgust. "They think you're the best thing to happen to this place in a long time." Her gaze falls to her hands, and I notice she's twisting her wedding ring. "People used to think that about me. About my family. We've done a lot for our community. Sacrificed our time. Given back without asking for anything in return." She pauses her movements, setting her palms flat against her thighs. "Now, you come in and think you can take my place? Be better than me? Run the PTA?" Rebecca scoffs.

"You told the news station who I was." It isn't a question, and her sly smile is all the answer I need. *Bitch.* I lick my lower lip and try not to crack a sarcastic smile. "You think I asked to become a super because I wanted to run the PTA?" Rebecca glances up from her hands. "You're pathetic, Rebecca."

"No, Jane. What's pathetic is you throwing yourself onto every news station within fifty miles. Someone like *you* taking care of this place?" She sways her head. "It's absolutely ridiculous."

"And you think you can do better? Save more people? By what... throwing money at them? Because that's all *you're* good for."

Rebecca's nose flares and her cheeks take on a soft pink hue. I've ruffled her, even if only a bit, but I cock an eyebrow in satisfaction.

"If you're just here to complain about the PTA and—"

"We've concluded our voting. By the way." She picks invisible link from her blouse. "Sorry to give you the bad news, but I will be remaining as president, *without* a vice president as my aid. We all agreed it was for the best with you being…" she flutters a single hand at me. "Preoccupied and all."

I gape. "How could you have voted without the entire PTA present?"

"It hasn't gone unnoticed that you've been absent lately." She shrugs.

"I was—and *am*—in the hospital!" I argue, but it's no use. Not when it comes to Rebecca.

Her lips purse slightly as if trying to contain a victorious smirk. "I didn't come here to debate, I came to deliver the news." She stands. "And to see your face when I told you that you lost, Jane." Rebecca leans her palms onto the mattress, coming closer. "And that if you fight back, I will bring you down. Just like this time and every time before when you tried to rise above me."

I don't know what she's talking about, as I've never ran against her for anything before, but the underlying threat doesn't go unnoticed. We watch each other, calculating each other's next moves. But Rebecca has a perfect poker face and doesn't flinch. The door opens and the nurse from earlier enters. He stops when he notices us in a paused discussion.

"Sorry," he says with a smile. "I need to check her vitals."

"It's fine. Rebecca was just leaving, actually."

Rebecca straightens and walks toward the exit. "Just remember, Jane. One powerful woman can make a difference, but two powerful women can begin a war. Whether that be as friends or between each other as enemies."

When the click of her heels quiets, the nurse shudders. "Well, that was unnerving. What did she mean by that?"

I sway my head, laying against the pillow. "No idea." But really, I have a sinking feeling Rebecca is going to do everything she can to ensure I don't take her spotlight. As the nurse begins checking my vitals, I stare into his hazel eyes. "So much for that list, huh?"

His face reddens, and he does everything to avoid eye contact as he concludes his check up. "It won't happen again," he says, exiting and clicking the door shut behind him.

CHAPTER 20

After two more days in the hospital, I'm released. Getting to the van and home was tricky as people—fans, I guess—were waiting to catch a glimpse of me, take photos, or who knows what else. We only had a few flashes of cameras that will be ugly exit shots.

"Do you want to settle on the couch, or can you make it upstairs?" Peter asks, setting my purse down on the counter.

I inhale the familiar scents of home and sigh. "I'm fine, Peter. Just sore is all."

He nods, tapping his fingers against the counter.

"What I could use is a hot shower, coffee, and donuts."

Peter chuckles. "That sounds fair. How about you get settled and I'll make a donut run?"

I crank the shower to the hottest setting, letting the steam waft around the bathroom, filling it with scents of eucalyptus and lemon, as I strip off my sweats. My supersuit was damaged during the explosion. I'll have to repair it somehow, but for now, I toss it into the hamper with the scrubs I borrowed from the hospital. With a heavy sigh, I step into the scalding shower, letting the burning water cleanse me of the event.

The entire scene plays out in my head. I had been so careful, so sure, that I could save the hostages. From what the news stations said, four hostages were killed in the explosion, plus the bomber, who was a disgruntled employee fired after working at the hotel for fifteen years, and one officer. Everyone else sustained burns or other wounds. I was lucky to have been down the hall when the bomb went off. Even so, I can't help but feel it's my fault they're all dead.

Six lives lost at my hand. Countless others hurt. The thought makes me tremble.

If I hadn't jumped in to help. If I had listened to the officer in command to stand down. If I had just let them do their *jobs*... perhaps some lives could have been saved.

My mind spins with the thought. Did I make the situation worse, or would it have played out in a similar fashion if I hadn't stepped in? Perhaps the assailant would have heard the team coming, gotten scared, and disarmed the bomb scared at the last second and given up. Maybe the officers could have *saved* the hostages... maybe there had been another way.

I sigh, leaning my head against the shower wall. Tears stream down my face, mixing with the water. By forcing my way into the situation, I only made it worse. They were right. I should have listened and waited, but my ego got the best of me and I thought I—Jane McKenna, some super who tried to rise above everyone—could handle the situation better than trained professionals? What was I thinking?

I stand under the cooling water, grieving those lost in the blast and letting the guilt wrap around inside my chest.

The problem was I *hadn't* been thinking... and now, not only will I have the scars to prove it, but an assigned officer at my door to ensure I don't leave, and a pending court date to review the case for my punishment.

With a heavy sigh, I turn the now cold water off, and slip into my coziest pajamas. A quick glance at the torn suit makes me wonder if I should ever put it back on again. Was I doing more harm than good? Was I wrong about everything it was to be a super? I ponder the questions as I slink downstairs. Peter is filling coffee mugs, a box of donuts on the counter beside him. The aroma of freshly brewed coffee and the promise of sugar relaxes me a bit, but still, worry clouds everything in my mind.

Peter hands me a mug and slides the donut box toward me. I select a maple bar and take a generous bite. The sugar melts on my tongue and I revel in the deliciousness. We each eat one in silence, and as I'm reaching for a sprinkle one next, Peter clears his throat.

"We should talk about what happened."

"I'd rather not," I say, not wanting to relive the moments again just yet. But the simple mention of it brings back a rush of heat to my body.

Peter screws his lips to the side and nods once. "We should at least discuss what happens next. Don't you think?"

"Probably." I sigh, sipping my coffee. It settles in my stomach with a sourness, doing nothing to make me feel better.

"The police chief sent over an officer to—"

"Babysit," I interrupt with a bite to my tone. "Yes, I know."

Peter exhales, running his fingers through his hair. "I'm not sure why you're mad about it. It's only fair." I glare at him. "You did insert yourself into a pretty serious police scene, Jane. Even after everyone told you not to."

"Thanks for the reminder," I snap, rolling my eyes. "Like I don't already feel enough guilt, I don't need the sting of the dagger pushed harder by you." I move to get up and leave the kitchen, but Peter reaches for me, taking my hand.

"You made a mistake. *Everyone* makes mistakes, Jane. Super or not. Hell, even in those movies we watch with Max, the good guys get in trouble sometimes, too. You thought you were doing the right thing,

I understand that, but the truth is, not everyone sees your actions as heroic. They see them as idiotic and attention grabbing."

I stare at him, not knowing how to respond to that brutal honesty. Before I can think of how to respond, the doorbell rings. Peter squeezes my hand then releases it, sliding from the stool with a groan of annoyance.

"It's probably another reporter. I'll send them away." He kisses my cheek before heading to the door.

As I sip my coffee, I hear voices from the entry. It doesn't sound like Peter is turning away reporters; it sounds like he's conversing with someone. I close my eyes and tune my attention toward the door.

Shit. Stay calm. They don't know anything for certain. Peter's mind is a jumble of worry.

He's hiding something. That woman is his wife. He did something with the compound.

The compound? I jump from my seat and find Peter at the door speaking with two men.

"Peter? What's going on?" I ask, and all eyes land on me. The two men are wearing suits and hold expressions of annoyance and distrust. "Who are these people?" My stomach sinks. Could they be agents of some secret super society like in Marvel? Here to recruit me for their team of special humans? Detectives to arrest me for the bombing? I've not a clue!

Peter deflates, standing aside to introduce the two men. "This is Dr. Zhao and Professor Ishida. They're from MSAD."

I shook him a look of confusion. The name is familiar, but—

"They sent the compound I've been studying," he interjects my thoughts.

I lick my lower lip. *Shit.* "Right. Hello." I give them a small wave.

Dr. Zhao eyes me suspiciously. He's an older gentleman with salt and pepper hair cut short around the ears. Clasping his hands behind his back, he looks at Peter, who gives him a single nod. Peter closes the door behind them as they enter the home. "We are hoping to gain answers regarding the tests."

"Specifically, the human trials," Professor Ishida adds, his almond eyes looking me over from head to toe.

"I-I'm not sure I know what you're talking about." Peter rubs the back of his neck and gives an awkward chuckle. "We've sent along all our findings so far—"

Dr. Zhao raises a hand, halting Peter mid sentence. "We've seen the news, Professor McKenna," he says, glancing in my direction. "It's not every day a super shows up in the same area we have sent a specialized compound to for testing."

Damn. Of course they figured out who I was. I used my own name on my costume. I said I wasn't going to hide... so why am I shocked that they knew it was me?

"You better come in and get comfortable," I remark, folding my arms over my chest. Peter gives me a wide stare. "What? Clearly, they've assumed what happened here. It's not like we can hide it. We might as well entertain them. They made a long trip to see me." With that, I turn and stalk toward the kitchen to prepare a tray of snacks and coffee.

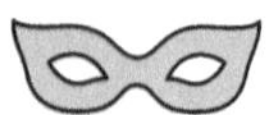

"So the compound was not injected? It was directly ingested?" Professor Ishido wonders, tapping his finger on the side of his mug. He's staring at his notebook where he's been taking diligent notes during the conversation. Peter and I explained what had happened and how it altered my senses. We shared the data of the cells and everything we could, all while Dr. Zhao stared at me in awe.

"Yes. Like I said, it was an accident. I thought it was Gatorade." I shrug, giving a nervous chuckle.

Professor Ishido sets his mug down and continues his notations. While the silence fills the space, I check my phone. It's almost time to get the kids from school and we need to wrap up the conversation before then.

Peter notices my unease and sets a hand on my knee.

"The kids?" I whisper.

"Cheyanne is going to Megan's for dinner, so she won't be home for a bit and Rebecca offered to give Max a ride home."

"Rebecca?" I blanch, raising my voice. The two men raise their gazes to me and I shrink back on the couch, lowering my voice. "Why would *she* offer?"

Peter's brows furrow. "I thought you two were friends now. She's been really helpful in bringing Max home when I can't for the last few days."

In all the craziness, I forgot to mention the conversation—and threats—from Rebecca's visit to the hospital. I worry my bottom lip, wondering what lies Rebecca is filling Max's head with. Max knows not to divulge information about my powers, but he's only ten, and things slip out without thinking.

"Is there a problem?"

"Uh, no, Dr. Zhao. But if you'll excuse us for a second," I say with a smile and motion for Peter to follow me to the kitchen.

Once we are alone, I tug him close and speak quietly, explaining what transpired between Rebecca and I.

"She's out for something. Information. Fame. I don't know." I flutter my hands.

Peter sighs. "I think you're over-exaggerating. She's head of the PTA and runs the classroom carpool for Max and Sterling's class. You really think she'd use a ten-year-old to get back at you? That's low, even for someone like her, if what you say is true."

"I don't know, Peter. She was seriously pissed about everything. She wants me to back down. Give up and take my place at the end of the table again. Quietly. Let her rule over the PTA alone."

Peter leans against the counter, crossing his arms over his chest. "I think you're looking into this a bit too deeply. I'm sure she didn't mean any of the sort."

"You weren't there. You don't know her like I do, Peter. She wants to ruin me... somehow."

"So, what are you going to do? Let her win?"

I toss my head back and groan. "I don't know." My eyes are tired and I feel a headache coming on. All of this is overwhelming. "I can't do anything right now. I can't just go back out there and pretend she didn't *threaten* me."

"It didn't sound like a genuine threat to me."

"I think we need to let all of this settle." I sigh, raking my hands down my face.

"That's probably a good idea," a voice from the entryway chimes. Turning, I notice Professor Ishido watching us. "Sorry, I was looking for the restroom. I didn't mean to overhear." He takes a step into the kitchen. "But I believe you are right to step back. We need to run some tests. Compare those with lab tests on the compound itself."

"Well," Peter begins, pressing from the counter. "Like we said, we don't have isolated compound samples anymore."

Professor Ishido smirks. "It is a good thing we brought some, then."

CHAPTER 21

After a few days recovering in the house, I finally get the courage to peek outside. The lawn is empty, but officers flank the porch.

My protection detail. I scoff knowing that they're here to make sure I don't leave the house. Protection of myself... or some shit.

The road is quiet, but two strange cars are parked along the block. They could be reporters or fans waiting for me to shuffle out in my slippers and robe, or they could be visiting the neighbors. Either way, I replace the curtains with a sigh.

Cheyanne has been unusually helpful, offering to drive to the store or watch TV with me. She passed her licensing exam and has been taking the van to and from school, but with everything going on, we've kept the kids home for anything else.

Max has been oddly quiet. Holed up in his room or sneaking about the kitchen for snacks when he thinks we aren't busy. I approached him yesterday, wondering if something was going on, but he insisted he was just tired and wanted to read in his room. The fact that he's not his usual perky self, especially when Dr. Zhao and Professor Ishido come by doesn't settle well with me, but Peter reminds me he is a growing boy and maybe the kids at school have been bombarding him with super questions. I agree. Home must be the only quiet place for everyone.

I haven't put on my suit yet, not that I could because it's in ruins, but the news has been especially curious as to why I haven't shown my face since the explosion. The requests for me to come out and say hi have dwindled, but according to Cheyanne, there are fan pages and cartoon sketches of me floating around the internet now.

With a groan, I turn on the TV flipping through the news stations for my daily check of, well, me. Pausing at the local station, I wait for the weather and watch the local events list scroll by. And then, the usual reporters show up.

"This just in," the female reporter says with a serious expression. "A woman, presumably another super, is on Main Street calling out our very own P.S. Jane."

I edge forward. What the hell is going on?

The male reporter adds, "I don't know if I'd call her a super, Margret, but she's definitely looking for attention. We have Joe on the scene now."

The screen changes to a man wearing a red coat standing on the sidewalk. A row of shops stretches behind him, and I recognize where he is. Main Street shopping district.

"Thank you, Margret and Steve. Yes. I'm here on Main Street, trying to determine exactly what is going on. So far, we know a woman has appeared, demanding that P.S. Jane comes out of hiding. Apparently, she wants to... talk?" he states, as if he isn't sure either. "Authorities have closed off the entire area, and local shops have locked their doors until we know more."

His picture flickers and a heavy gale whips around the reporter. The camera shakes and the TV fills with sounds of wind. My stomach knots and I grip my chest. Something is wrong.

A shriek pierces through the noise, and the camera pivots to find a woman wearing a tight black leotard with green embroidery. Her long inky hair is braided over her shoulder, barely affected by the breeze. The mask on her face is thick and shiny, like plastic.

She's standing in the middle of the street. Thrusting her arms out to the side, she releases a scream that rushes from her like a sonic wave. Windows shatter, tossing glass outward in tiny pieces.

The camera drops to the ground, but doesn't stop recording.

When the scream quiets, the air fills with a blast of wind. It picks up the glass, swirling it like a deadly storm. Dark heeled boots step closer to the camera, and then the woman is bending down, peering into the lens. She taps manicured nails against the glass.

"Janie," her voice coos, dripping with venom. "Come out, come out, wherever you are."

A shudder overtakes me.

"Every day you don't show yourself, I'll destroy another street of this perfect town you claim to love so much," she continues. "It won't take long to bring this entire place down. It is a *quaint* little area, after all." She chuckles, but I find no humor in the tone. The voice is familiar, but I can't place where I know it from. That fact niggles at the back of my mind. *Think, Jane. Think!*

What I do know is that this is no new super. This is a villain.

Peter exits his office, slamming the door behind him. "We have a problem." He isn't looking at me, but at the phone in his hand.

"Yes. We do." My eyes are glued to the screen.

"Someone broke into the lab. I have to get to the university."

I gape at him. "What? How? I thought they increased security recently?"

Peter's head shakes. "It's a small town university. There's only so much security we can provide. There were extra university security officers on patrol, but..." he sighs, rubbing the back of his neck. "It isn't a government lab with trained professionals with high security clearance. With the right keycard or ID badge, the officers would have let them in."

"But the compound... wasn't it in a locked compartment?"

He nods. "Someone picked the lock... broke the glass... I'm not sure. I won't know until I get there. Security and Dr. Zhao are waiting for me." I hear his keys jingle, but his footsteps halt on their way to the door. "What's going on?"

I glance at him. Peter is staring at the TV Shifting on the couch, I exhale sharply through my nose. "I think whoever broke into your lab drank that compound. There's a new villain in town."

Fuck. Peter's thoughts cloud my mind with curses and worry.

"I-I have to go. Dr. Zhao—"

I wave him off. "Go."

"You sure?" His eyes flicker over me with concern, but I nod.

"Be careful," I warn, knowing that if this woman discovered the compound, she must know a lot about my family. Not that the news hasn't been helpful there, spewing facts about the McKenna crew to every station, but something about this woman is familiar and sends a tingling warning through my body.

"Cheyanne!" I call, hurrying up the stairs. Her door opens, and she gives me a strange look of confusion. "I need your help."

With Cheyanne's support, and the aid of Prime delivery, we are able to piece my suit together. It's not perfect, but the torn and burned areas are patched. It goes on with ease, and I realize after being in the hospital and moping about at home, I've actually lost some weight. The suit fits comfortably—*more* so than before.

Cheyanne takes in my reflection beside me and nods. "It looks good. *You* look good, mom."

"Thank you for your help," I say, turning to her. "I couldn't have figured all this out without you." I reach for her hand and she lets me grasp it. We exchange warm smiles and then I tug her in for a hug. Cheyanne doesn't fight me. Instead, she wraps her arms around me and squeezes right back.

"Are you sure you want to do this?"

Drawing away, I observe her face. My daughter, the one who's been adamant about this whole thing being insane, is concerned.

"No." I chuckle dryly. "I'm not sure. And honestly, it's terrifying, but we have to jump into scary things to get over our fears. Right?"

She nods. "And you're sure you don't need us?"

I purse my lips to the side. "No. I want you to stay here with Max. If anything goes wrong, you have to be here for each other."

"And what about dad? He's usually in your ear."

"He'll be too busy at the university. Besides, I have someone perfect for the job."

CHAPTER 22

I'm sweating more than I'd like to admit. If I raise my arms high enough, it will be obvious how nervous I am. It's been two days since the new villain, claiming to be called B.B. has threatened the town, and so far she's made good on those intimidations, destroying the entirety of what once was Main Street and part of the next.

Walking down the center of the road, I examine what's left of the buildings. Every window sits shattered, shards fill the sidewalks like glitter. The smell of smoke wafts around me and I notice a few openings—whether windows or doors—rimmed with soot. It looks like menacing darkness oozing from inside. Staring long enough makes it appear as though it *is* actually moving.

I shake off the desolate feeling creeping over me and tune my thoughts into anyone that may be nearby. So far, everything has been silent. So quiet, it feels unnatural.

"Everything good, boss?" Lynn's voice whispers through the Bluetooth. More than eager to take part in our plan tonight, she hurried to my house, snacks in hand, ready to be my person in the chair. I'm confident in her aid. She's a wiz at Google and can channel surf like the best of them. Knowing Lynn will monitor the news and any events that pop up online about what's about to transpire makes me feel calmer. Plus, having an adult in the house with my kids is comforting.

"Yeah," I breathe. "No sign of her yet."

"Copy that!" Her voice is sharp and chipper.

I've made it to the end of the street. Turning to the right, I head to Second Street, where B.B. has last been seen. I walk cautiously, eyes scanning the road for any kind of movement. Shadows glide across a few windows. I notice there are people on the second story where a handful of apartments line the street.

"Shit."

"What's going on? What happened?" Lynn immediately interjects.

I worry my bottom lip. "There's still people here. The apartments above some stores."

"Why haven't they evacuated?"

I shrug, then remember she can't see me. "I don't know. Maybe they have nowhere else to go."

"Right. I'll see what I can do." The line goes quiet and I'm again left with the buzzing in my ears.

The scent of a freshly lit match greets me, and I follow the aroma. I pause before a candle shop, staring into the windows. I see a small fire catching rapidly.

"Lynn, there's a fire at Lit & Flame."

"On it."

I trust she's calling the fire department, but right now, something else draws my attention.

That bitch. The familiar voice greets me internally, and then I hear the click-clack of heels against pavement. Whipping around, my gaze lands on her. B.B. My very own villain.

Finally, she thinks, and a sneer spreads across her darkened lips. Her outfit looks flawless, like a mix of Cat Woman and Black Widow. Deadly, fierce, and poisonous. Plus, B.B. is slim and looks the part, unlike me.

We stalk toward each other as flames billow behind me. I feel like I'm in an action movie where things are always blowing up behind the hero, but I pray the shop doesn't explode. I've been in one bomb already. I don't need to be tossed about twice from a fiery explosion. I don't believe my back could take it.

"Hello, P.S. Jane." She articulates my name in disgust. "Nice of you to come out and meet me."

Standing a car's length apart, we both halt. "Sorry, I was indisposed to come sooner," I joke with a half-hearted shrug. "Some of us have been taking care of this town, not destroying it."

B.B. scoffs. "Don't pretend like you actually *care* about this place. We all know you're just doing this for attention."

I roll my eyes. "What's your motive for destroying it, then? Huh?"

"To draw you out."

"Why?"

She cocks her head. "Because people like you don't deserve to rule places like this."

I flex my fingers at my side, ready and waiting to punch this bitch in the face. "People like me?"

Her dark eyes trail over my body before she raises a single brow. "Yeah. People. Like. You. Those who think just because they can do something others can't makes them special. Gives them the right to squish those above them. To take power they don't *deserve*." She's talking through her teeth, frustration building within her.

I try to tune into her mind. Rolling thoughts of taking me down filter through my thoughts. I blink them away. Some are gruesome, painful, or totally unreal. She's here to harm me. That much is clear.

"Isn't that what you're doing? Taking power you don't deserve?" I take a single step toward her. "You stole the compound from the lab, but

I wonder, who told you about it?"

A wicked smirk teases her lips. "Someone vulnerable. Bendable. All too trusting of adults."

My brows furrow, and I think over the last few days. The only people I'd been in contact with are in my house. Cheyanne has been overly helpful. Perhaps the guilt of spilling my secrets drew her to my side. But she's been taking care of herself. The only adults she's been in contact with are her teachers, as far as I know.

I narrow my gaze at the woman before me. My gut tells me I know exactly who this is and I don't believe it's one of Cheyanne's teachers.

That only leaves...

"Max," I say his name in a whisper, but B.B. chuckles. I've hit the mark.

Max has been oddly quiet and reserved. And has been in close quarters with—

"Rebecca."

B.B. winks. "That's right, *Janie*. And it's time you understand your place in this town. There can only be one Bad Bitch here, and that's me."

"Bad Bitch?" I snark. "Is that what the B.B. stands for? I thought it was *Basic* Bitch."

Rebecca snarls, then takes a length inhale, spreading her arms out to her side. The air rushes by me, surrounding Rebecca in a cloud of haze and debris. I stumble back a step, struck by her power. If the compound gave me abilities, of course it would give *her* some too.

With a sharp exhale, the gale charges me. It hits me with a force I'd imagine a car would have and knocks me off my feet. I spiral through the air, hitting the concrete with a generous *thunk*. But the wind doesn't stop there, it continues to force me back. I claw at the rough ground, trying to find purchase as I slide down the street on my stomach closer to the flaming shops.

Finally, I find a crack in the road and grip hard. Thank goodness for my strength, otherwise, she'd have blown me right into a billowing building.

Blinking through the debris, I see Rebecca hovering a foot above the ground, floating toward me with ease.

"Wind power," I shout. "Cool party trick. Did you get the hover boots from some swanky inventor?"

Tipping her head back, Rebecca cackles. "Oh, Janie. These aren't hover boots, but my suit, well, that's all Prime. *You* taught me that, didn't you? What did you say?" She taps her chin in consideration, drifting nearer. "You can Prime anything. Well, I Primed myself a whole supersuit, and even these boots." Lifting one leather boot, she smiles. I hate to admit it, but they are cute and fitting for her wicked appearance.

The hurricane doesn't ease. Instead, it closes in tighter, pressing against me from all sides. Even though I'm surrounded by air, I can't catch my breath. The oxygen seems unwilling to enter my body, and I gasp in desperation.

"Oh, this won't be so fun if you pass out already!"

The zephyr slows enough for me to relax my grip and suck in a deep breath. My heart is pounding so hard I can feel it thump throughout my entire body.

"Fun?" Drawing my knees under me, I rise gradually and shake out the cramp in my fingers. "What exactly are you hoping for here, Becca?"

"A little revenge... a little bit of showing you who really runs this place." She cracks her knuckles and rolls her neck. "You don't deserve to be in charge around here. You haven't worked for it like I have." She steps toward me. "I've done the ground work. I've been there for this town. I've sacrificed so much for this community. And you..." she scoffs. "You think you can put on a tacky suit and be handed the keys to the kingdom? I. Think. Not."

Reaching for my Bluetooth, I realize it's gone. The fall must have dislodged it from my ear, and at this rate, it could be anywhere. Flashing lights pierce through the smoke behind Rebecca, and a quick glance over my shoulder shows another set of police cars closing off this end of the street. My head spins with dizziness as thoughts collide through my mind. Concerns from the officers, relaying messages, and instructions cloud my thoughts. I close my eyes for an instant to force them out until I'm met with my trembling worries.

Even with my strength and mind reading, can I overpower Rebecca? I lift my gaze to hers. She's watching me, hands at the ready by her side. There's no one else coming. No one else is going to swoop in and help me. I have to do this on my own. I have to take out Rebecca and prove that I can help this community... even with my mistakes in the past. This is my moment because no one else has the ability to take her on. Not the police. Not the MASD. Just me.

I notice a mail drop box to my right. Without hesitation, I run to it, yank it from its hold and toss it at Rebecca. She deflects it with a flick of her hand; the wind carrying it up and over her without harm. Rebecca's stare follows the mailbox, and I use that tiny distraction to charge her.

I barrel into her, colliding so hard she lets out an *oomph*. We crash into the road, skidding a few feet before stopping. In an instant, Rebecca is inhaling, opening her mouth, and releases a shriek so loud it sends me faltering. Still straddling Rebecca, I grip my ears. The noise is deafening and unbalancing. I stumble to the side, feeling as though the road is undulating beneath me. Out of the corner of my eyes, I see Rebecca stagger to her knees. Out of breath, the scream has stopped, but my brain is left spinning and ears are ringing.

A rumble draws both our attention up. Through the growing smoke, a helicopter whirls, clearing some of the haze. A camera points out the side window as it hovers above us and I imagine this scene playing live on the local news.

Rebecca is on her feet and rises on the collecting wind.

"No," I shout, but it's too late. Rebecca shoves her arms up and the gale follows, whipping itself into the helicopter and tossing it off kilter. I stumble to my feet, wobbling to Rebecca, pressing through the torrent of air. When I reach her, there's a calmness. She is the eye of the storm and nothing seems to touch her here. With her gaze fixed on forcing the helicopter away, I throw my arms around her. The gesture is shocking, causing her to falter and the hurricane to change course. It tears into a building and the flames race along the breeze, creating a cloud of fire that almost catches the helicopter. I glance up and watch it veer to avoid it.

"Let me go!" Rebecca tries to alter the surrounding air, but I reach up and grab her arms one at a time, pinning them to her side. I'm embracing her tightly, and she can only take shallow breaths. Not enough to banshee scream at me again. Frustration clouds her features, and she grunts, kicking against me to get away. But what she doesn't realize is that I'm stronger than she knows.

"I don't only hear thoughts, *Becca*," I brag. "I'm also really, really strong." To prove my point, I squeeze tighter. Rebecca's face contorts into discomfort.

"I know. Max told me," she jests, trying to rile me up more. It works, and my arms close in around her more... and more. I can see a slight panic in her eyes. "What are you going to do, Jane? Crush me to death?" she blusters, licking her lower lip. "Just remember, everyone watching will only remember you by your next action." Her eyes flicker to the helicopter that has returned, hovering above us, recording our moves. "No matter what you do, though, you'll still be that pathetic mom in carpool dreaming of being someone like *me*."

I shake my head. "I don't want to be like you, Rebecca. Why would I?" And then I realize what she's doing; goading me into submission, wanting to make me feel bad about myself, make myself feel small. At one time, that may have worked, toying with my emotions and feeling of inadequacy, but now, I've embraced who I am and nothing will stop me from proving I am capable. "Why don't you admit that you're just like me?"

Rebecca glares. "I'm *nothing* like you," she spits. "I have everything I want."

"Then why are you fighting so hard to be *like me*?"

Her eyes flutter and her mouth opens as if in shock. "N-no. That is *not*—" She jerks against my hold and this time I release her and watch as she lurches back a step. Rubbing her arms, she sways her head.

"You manipulated my son to tell you about the compound. A child! Something I'd never do. But you drank the compound to develop abilities, like me. And you're out here *threatening* me and the town just to what? Take my place as the local super? Sounds like you want what I have, Rebecca."

"I have more than you'll ever have. I have a say in this place. Power and sway over decisions made. But you?" She scoffs, fluttering her hands at me. "You're just a PTA mom who barely has time to make the effort to *show up*."

I shake my head. "You're wrong. I have a family who thrives here. A friend who would do anything for me. A town who... at the moment may hate me, but eventually will see that I do want to help them. Why do you think I want to help build the PTA into something better? I want to make this a place for our kids to grow with, to show them how to care for those around them and their community." The air builds around me when I take a step toward her. "I didn't notice it before because I always pegged you as an entitled bitch."

Rebecca's lips curl into a snarl and the wind bats against me. "Didn't notice what?"

"That you're just as lonely and lost as I have been."

The gale dies, but only for an instant. Then Rebecca is reeling back, throwing a punch right to my jaw. With the power of the zephyr behind the hit, I'm tossed back, flipping, and landing on my stomach. It knocks the wind from my lungs and loose gravel scratches at my cheek.

"That's not true," Rebecca shouts from above me.

I cough, peering at her. Rebecca's eyes are watchful and angry, but I can see the mistiness in them because there's truth in what I've said.

Pressing to my knees, I sit on my heels and stare at her. "There's nothing wrong with feeling lonely," I tell her, brushing the debris from my palms. "It's hard making friends as moms. I thought *we* were becoming friends." I lift my shoulders in a shrug. "And then I realized you were just using me."

Her lips purse to the side, and she lowers to glower over me. "We were never friends."

I sigh, then in a single motion, reach out and lock my fingers around her ankle, jerking her down. Unprepared for the sudden jest, Rebecca's arms windmill and her head cracks against the cement. I pause, watching to make sure I didn't hurt her more than I intended, but I see her chest rise and fall. She lets out a groan.

Rebecca scoots into a seated position, and I shuffle to my feet. Reaching to the back of her head, she draws her hand away smeared with blood. When her eyes land on me, I can feel their loathsomeness burn through me.

"You weren't always such a bitch, Rebecca. What happened to you?"

I wonder, remembering a time when she was cordial and friendly toward everyone in the PTA.

"What happened to me?" she sneers, using the wind to propel herself to her feet. She lands unsteadily. "You happened to me!" Rebecca thrusts her hands out toward me and a blast of air shoves me back. "You took my spotlight." Another gust and I skid, almost stumbling to the ground. "You wanted to take my place!" Her voice rises, cracks with anger against the current of air. "Everyone likes you, Jane. You're *relatable*," she says with disgust. "You're *normal*. You're... P.S. Jane." Each word spits like venom from her mouth. "Who wouldn't want a supermom to run this place? To watch over the town and the schools." Thrusting her hands once more, I'm hit with a blast, like a slap in the face. "Even after the disaster you caused at the hotel, people are talking about *you!*"

"I've only ever helped you," I shout, not realizing how much anger I've been holding in against her. "I gave you ideas. I gave you *help* when you needed it. I didn't want to steal your spotlight. I only wanted a place where I felt like I belonged. You have only ever been a bitch to me. Making me feel inadequate and small-minded. I realize now you only ever did it to make yourself seem big. To make yourself feel important. You enjoy control, Becca, but you can't control me."

Rebecca inhales, winding up for a blaring banshee scream, but I rush her, wrapping my arms around her waist and tackling her to the ground. She struggles against my hold, but I'm much stronger than her and pin her arms over her head.

"Stop fighting me!" I wince as she whips her knee into my back, but I refuse to let go. "Stop it!" I shout, shaking her. Understanding she won't be able to escape my hold, Rebecca puffs out a breath and glares daggers at me. "When will you realize you're not alone?"

Rebecca blinks, and her features soften into confusion. "But I am."

"Only because you've made it that way. You've pushed everyone in your life away from you."

"That's not true!" she laments.

"It is." I squeeze her wrists, and she winces. "Being a mom is hard. Especially when you have no one in your corner. But if we stick together, it makes life easier." I pause, catching my breath. "Everyone needs help sometimes. Me running for vice president was not me trying to take your place. Maybe at first it was, but then I realized I wanted to be your partner, to bring new light to the group, make this place the best. Don't you understand that?"

Rebecca is quiet for a moment. Her eyes drift above me to where the helicopter is still hovering, recording. When she looks back at me, she deflates. "My husband is leaving me."

"W-what?" My grip loosens. Sure, I had joked about her husband cheating on her, but I didn't think it was actually *true*. Guilt washes over me for not seeing the truth behind my words earlier.

Turning her head away, she nods. "Apparently, he's been sleeping with some woman he met on one of his business trips."

"Rebecca, I'm so sorry. I didn't know... I mean, I wasn't sure..." I stammer.

"No one does." She sniffs.

I release her, shifting so I'm kneeling next to her. Rebecca sits, rubbing her wrists.

"It's been... difficult. Balancing everything. The court dates, the lawyers, the programs I lead, the PTA..." she adds, glancing at me with remorse.

"I can't even imagine." I place my hand on her shoulder and a tiny smile crosses her face. "You know, you have people in your corner. People who you can talk to."

"You said it yourself. Everyone hates me." Her confession comes out low and shaky. "I wasn't lying when I said everyone prefers you. I thought if the compound had made you so sure and confident that maybe—" she cuts herself off, shaking her head.

"You thought it could help you, too," I conclude for her. "But, Rebecca, what you don't realize is that it wasn't just the compound that brought all that about. Sure, it helped kick my ass into gear, but it was me realizing that I was more capable than I thought. It forced me to dig deep and accept who I am without changing myself. It brought me closer to my family. Made me see what was really important in my life. This superhero stuff... I do it because I can. Because the compound gave me the powers I have. It's kind of just a bonus." I chuckle.

"I thought they'd make me better. Make people notice me."

"Well," I snort. "People did notice you." Tilting my head back, I stare at the helicopter, giving them a small wave. When I return my attention to Rebecca, she has her knees drawn to her chest. "With your abilities, you could have worked *with* me. Why did you decide to be the villain?"

Resting her chin on her knees, Rebecca stares at the ground. "You said it yourself, I've always been the bitch."

"Are you willing to let that all go?"

Her eyes meet mine, and she gives a small nod.

"Then let's get out of here." I stand, offering her my hand. She takes it and I pull her to her feet. We stand there, watching each other, unsure if we can trust the other isn't about to begin another smack down. Then Rebecca exhales, drooping her shoulders. I take the moment to wrap my arms around her, embracing her like a friend. Only, I'm a bit too enthusiastic because I hear her struggle to catch her breath, and then she passes out in my arms.

CHAPTER 23

Setting a vase of flowers on the bedside table, I take a seat, listening to the sound of machines beeping. Rebecca has only been here a day, but just like when I had been admitted, people have flocked to the hospital to see the villain unmasked.

Rebecca shifts, fluttering her eyes open. When she notices me, she smiles. "Hey," she says groggily, pressing into a seated position.

"How are you feeling?"

"Sore. Headache. Nothing too horrible." We share a soft chuckle. "Thanks for the flowers."

I smile. "You're welcome."

A petite nurse comes in, quietly checking vitals and adjusting numbers on the machines Rebecca is hooked up to. "You should be able to leave tomorrow morning if the officers let you," the woman explains. "Don't forget to order lunch. Today is lasagna day and, to be honest, it's delicious." With that, she exits, leaving us surrounded in silence once more.

With a sigh, I lean my elbows on my knees. "I'm sorry about everything you're going through." Rebecca waves it off like it's no big deal. "Really. I am. Going through a divorce and juggling your son and all the activities you do... I'm sure it's difficult."

Rebecca nods, staring at her hands in her lap. "How is Sterling?"

"He's fine. Your mom is caring for him. I checked in on him at school yesterday. He seems okay. Misses you, but your mom said she'd bring him by this evening."

"Good. Good." She shifts, wincing. "I miss that brat." Her laugh is genuine. Short, but joyful. "Do you think…" she pauses with a sniff. When her eyes meet mine they're filled with concern. "Do you think they'll let him stay with me? After all this?"

"I'm not sure," I admit. "You have a court date set, don't you? You can plead your case then. Maybe they'll go easy on you." My voice is small but hopeful. Rebecca made some shitty choices and caused a lot of damage around the community, but before all this, the town knew her as a genuine do-gooder. Perhaps they'll go easy on her… one can only hope for the sake of her kid.

With a nod, Rebecca opens a small menu from her tray and scans it. "Ugh, everything on here is at least 1200 calories, I'm sure. Good thing I can eat anything without worrying about that now, though."

"What?" I furrow my brows. That's an odd thing to say.

Rebecca shrugs. "One of my abilities. I can eat anything without feeling bloated or gross. I imagine I won't gain any weight either."

I snort. "How the hell did you figure that out?"

"After I drank the compound and woke up with a nasty hangover, all I wanted was a fat cheeseburger and fries. Of course, I ate an entire meal of it, and normally I'd feel bloated and greasy afterwards, but I felt energized and satiated. So I kept testing what I could eat. So far, nothing seems to bother me."

"You lucky bitch," I guffaw. "I wish I had that ability! I look at a plate of brownies and gain two pounds." That makes Rebecca laugh too. "Are those your only powers? Wind. The scream. Food."

"As far as I can tell. The scream thing was wild. I almost busted all the windows in our house yelling at Sterling to pick up his Lego city in the living room. How about you? What else can you do besides hug a person unconscious?"

I wince. "Sorry about that." Taking a long inhale, I relax into the chair. "Strength, mind reading, and I only need like two hours of sleep a night."

"Shut up! Now that is lucky. Can you imagine the kind of things we could accomplish if we didn't need to *sleep?*"

"I do, actually."

Rebecca orders her lunch and settles on the bed. She side-eyes me before finding the remote.

"You don't have to stay," she says, turning on the T.V.

"I know. I want to, though."

"Why?"

I scratch my chin, pursing my lips to the side. "Well, after everything that happened, you could use someone on your side. You don't seem to have a lot of friends." The honesty makes her wince. "And plus, I know what you're going through."

"Being nice even after I was such a bitch to you?"

I nod. "Everyone deserves a second chance."

Rebecca considers this, staring at the buttons on the remote. She exhales sharply, leaning her head against the pillow. "I don't think I do. But thank you."

I watch as she flips through the channels, avoiding the news stations as much as possible, featuring footage from our fight. She pauses at Food Network, setting the remote beside her.

"I love Food Network," I remark.

"Oh, me too. The cupcake battles are my favorite."

We look at each other, realizing that we, in fact, do have quite a bit in common.

"I love those, too."

Rebecca gives me a friendly smile. "You know, Jane. I've been think-ing. It would be nice to have someone helping run the PTA. Not as a co-president, of course," she scoffs. "But I'd be honored if you were my vice president."

"Are you sure?"

She nods. "The parents need someone like you balancing someone like me. Working together on the projects, sharing our ideas... I think we could make a difference."

"I think so, too." I reach forward to grab her hand. "Thank you."

Rebecca presses her lips into a line. "And don't worry about me start-ing any fires or fights soon in that suit. I'll be too busy helping rebuild the disaster I made." She draws her hand away, tucking her loose hair behind her ear. I've never seen her so undone. It's comforting to know even Rebecca has frizz.

"I heard they have you on probation."

She nods. "Two years if I have a *positive attitude*, they told me. Com-munity service. Written apologies. House arrest when not attending said events."

"That's not too bad. It could be a lot worse. They could have tossed you in prison."

Rebecca lolls her head toward me. "Yeah, but it won't look good in court fighting for custody of Sterling. I'm sure my husband will use it against me."

I give her a sad smile. "It's going to be hard, but you will figure it all out. The Rebecca I know wouldn't let something like this break her."

Rebecca smirks. "Yeah, but can we talk about those suits? I don't know how you wear something like that. Talk about chaffing!"

I laugh deeply. "No more Bad Bitch?"

Her head sways. "I'm retiring my suit."

"We could team up on super stuff, too. I could use help keeping the town safe. Your abilities are amazing. Maybe we could call you the Basic Bitch. Then you wouldn't have to change the suit."

Rebecca stares at me, a slow smile spreading on her face. "Yeah? You'd want me to help you?"

"Why not? Two women fighting crime... we could be a powerhouse!"

"Thanks, Jane. I'd like that."

We watch the episode in silence until Rebecca's lunch arrives. She picks at it, taking petite bites, and halfway through she sets her fork down.

"Jane," Rebecca says, her voice soft. When I turn to her, she's staring at the plate. "I'm really sorry about using Max. You were right. It was a horrible thing for someone to do; manipulate a child."

"He felt guilty about telling you," I reply. "But we talked about it and he understands it wasn't his fault."

"Will you tell him I'm sorry?"

I nod. "You know, it's actually a good thing we are friends now." Rebecca shoots me a confused look. "When Sterling was over the other day, the two of them couldn't stop talking about us."

"Really?" Her eyes glisten with hope.

"Yeah. Two supermoms? What are the odds?" I smirk but wink. "I'm glad they're friends, too."

Rebecca's smile is surprisingly shy. "Sterling needs a friend like Max. He doesn't have a lot of kids to hang out with. I think that's partially my fault."

I shrug. "Sterling is a great kid. You've done well raising him."

"That means so much to me, Jane. Thank you."

The officer standing at her door pokes his head in letting me know my visiting time is up. I stand, gripping my purse handles tightly while I watch Rebecca. Her complexion is pale and dark bags hang under her eyes. I've never seen her so... human.

"When you're out of here and ready to talk... about the divorce or super stuff, give me a call. Okay?"

Rebecca brightens slightly. "I will. Thank you, Jane."

"Okay everyone, let's get started."

Rebecca stands at the front of the table wearing her iconic dark silk blouse. This time, she paired it with skinny jeans. Jeans! Something I'd never imagined Rebecca to wear. Her hair is loose and her face no longer is as pinched and judgemental as it usually is at PTA meetings. I'm slumped in my usual spot at the end of the table. Lynn sips her coffee beside me, waiting for the final votes of the PTA line up.

"As you know, we've had a lot happen over the last few weeks. I'm sorry I haven't been around as often, but there are some things going on that have drawn my attention away from our events." Rebecca sits, another behavior she doesn't normally have at meetings.

"Yeah, like starting fires," someone jokes.

The mention of her villany makes Rebecca turn red, but composed as ever, she doesn't let the comment derail her. Rebecca may still be under constant supervision—an officer is even present at the meeting today—but it hasn't stopped her from continuing her role as PTA president. After clearing her throat, she glances at the members around the table. "Some of you know I'm going through a divorce and, I'll be honest, it's taking a lot of my energy and attention."

"So sorry, Rebecca," someone remarks.

She smiles. "Thank you. But it'll be okay because not only did I ask Jane to step up and assist me, but you all voted her as our new vice president."

All eyes turn on me. Warmth floods my cheeks. Not because of all the attention, but because it is by Rebecca's hand. A few members clap, sharing friendly smiles.

"Jane will be the new vice president of the PTA. She will be my right-hand woman in all decisions and take my place when I need to be elsewhere." Rebecca's gaze lands on me and she shares a secret smile with me. "So, with that out of the way." She rubs her hands together, then opens a folder in front of her. "Stacy will remain as secretary. Michael will become our new treasurer."

"Way to go," Lynn says, nudging my shoulder after the meeting. "I don't know what you did, but Rebecca is a whole new person after... you know." She raises her eyebrows as if it's a secret Rebecca was the villain. Turns out, everyone discovered her identity right away. Just like the news blasted my name, they did so with Rebecca's as well. Turns out, being the wife of one of the most well-known lawyers in town makes it difficult to hide a secret identity. Especially when said lawyer is blabbing about it in court to fight for custody of Sterling and parental rights. So far, Rebecca has been able to sway the court in her favor, and Sterling has spoken up about wanting to stay with his mom. She may be on probation for the next few years, but hopefully she will have her son beside her to keep her balanced. I couldn't imagine losing custody of my child after everything. But that is a risk we take as supers... and villains.

I tilt my head. "Yeah. She is. I guess she just needed someone to knock her down a peg or two." I wink and we both chuckle.

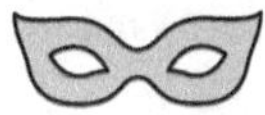

Dr. Zhao and Professor Ishido are here for another few days. Rebecca and I have both been in the lab providing samples of whatever they need. So far, they've been able to isolate the compound in our blood to determine how they can use it in other patients. Back at their headquarters, there are three terminal patients waiting for a miracle. Dr. Zhao hopes that with our help, they can find a solution to their cases, although the professor is worried about unintentionally creating more supers around the world.

"Whatever happens next," Dr. Zhao tells the professor. "It will be something unexpected. Possibly a miracle if we can find the right way to introduce the compound to the sick."

"I know you'll figure it out," I tell them, drawing my sleeve down from a recent blood draw. "And until you do, you know where to find us."

Professor Ishido nods, turning his back to label the samples.

"Promise me you'll continue to do good with what you've been given." Dr. Zhao grips my hands, a wistful smile on his lips. "Both of you." His eyes dart to Rebecca, who grins sheepishly.

She nods and I draw the doctor in for a hug.

"Thank you."

"No, Jane. Thank you. Without you, we never would have witnessed such an amazing transformation."

"I should go," Rebecca starts, buttoning her coat. "I have a meeting with the lawyer in a half hour."

"I'll walk out with you." I grab my jacket and zip it up. Giving Peter a quick kiss on the cheek, I follow Rebecca through the hallway and out onto the university walkway.

The air is warm today. Students meander through the lush grass and a few are laying on blankets with books out. Rebecca pauses, taking in the scene before us with a slow inhale. A gentle breeze wraps around us, bringing the scent of freshly cut grass and flowers with it.

"Careful or you'll cause a scene," I tease.

Rebecca smirks. "I've been practicing controlling how *much* air I'm moving." Her eyes are closed and her face tips toward the sky. "I love the feeling of the wind. It's freeing. Refreshing. Like mother nature wrapping her arms around me and letting me know everything will be okay."

Placing my hand on her shoulder, she peeks at me. "Everything *will* be okay. We're supers. Super*moms*. Nothing can stop us!"

A thought drifts from Rebecca's mind. *Thank you for being my friend.*

As I wrap my arm around her shoulder, I squeeze her gently. "Come on. We have a lot to do before our stakeout tonight."

EPILOGUE

"Hot dogs? Really?"

I turn to Rebecca, an eyebrow raised. "You said you can eat anything, right? And these are the best hot dogs you can find." We approach the small cart where a familiar face greets me.

"P.S. Jane! I was wondering when you'd visit me again." He's already preparing my usual order, and when he glances up while squeezing ketchup on, he beams. "And you brought a *friend*?" His pale eyes narrow as he takes in Rebecca. Recognition floods his facade and he hesitates to prepare our food.

"This is my new partner, B.B. She'll take a dog and a drink too, please."

Rebecca exhales through her nose, crossing her arms over her chest. "Make that two dogs, with mustard."

I pivot to face her. "Two?"

She shrugs. "I'm starving, and like you said, it's not like it's going to bother me."

"New partner, huh?" His lips purse, but after a moment, he nods once and continues his motions to prepare the food. "I'm Gus. Always here to help after hours." Gus winks, and I realize I've never asked him for his name before. It makes the whole exchange more intimate. Friendly and comforting.

I chuckle, then take my hot dog from Gus. "Thanks, Gus!"

When Rebecca has her order, we make our way back to the van and indulge on street food, Pepsi, and whatever chocolates I have stashed in the glove box. The police scanner buzzes to life a few times with a domestic disturbance, a stray pack of dogs, and one nude man walking down Washington Street.

"Think we will get any action tonight?" Rebecca wonders, dabbing mustard from the corner of her mouth.

I frown. "I hope so."

Although the police have given us a written notice to not overstep during hostile situations, they've agreed to allow us on the scene to aid *as needed*. We've helped with a few small tasks around the community, but have done our best to not interfere. So far, our probations have been lightened, Rebecca has partial custody of Sterling, and the townspeople are beginning to recognize how helpful we can be. I believe, in the future, we won't be trailed by our own personal police escorts—not for probationary reasons at least—and we can live our dual lives without too many hiccups. At least, that's my hope for Rebecca and I. To leave a legacy behind. To keep Brightwood safe. To ensure people see moms deeper than surface level. To know they are a force, an influence, and more than just chauffeurs.

The scanner comes to life reporting a tripped alarm at a jewelry store. Rebecca perks, clicking her seatbelt. She draws her mask down and glances at me. "Ready?"

I can't help but grin. Having a partner, someone as eager to jump into action as I am, feels amazing. Wonderful and enlightening and a little bit dangerous because who knows what kind of trouble two supers can cause? Let alone two super*moms* out on the prowl for crime.

"Ready. Let's hit it." With a curt nod, I peel out of the parking lot toward our destination.

— The End —

Acknowledgements

This novel has been in the works for many, many years. At first it was a joke between my husband and me, just a regular random car-trip conversation while trying to pass the time. Turns out, after writing a rough draft just for fun, we sparked something amazing! So a huge thanks to Doug, my husband, for helping craft the foundation of this story. Turns out, we make a pretty good team, huh? ;)

Angela, thank you for being my sounding board and always being willing to read all drafts I throw at you. You inspired the character Lynn, and of course, your famous cheesecake brownies got an honourable mention (which I'm still waiting for you to make me...) so thank you for allowing me to put a piece of you in here as well! You're wonderful!

Thank you, Caitlin, my editor, for working through the trenches of P.S. JANE. I'm sorry for all the ellipses, LOL, but I'm glad I could make you laugh! I'm so thankful to have met you and can't wait to continue working with you in the future.

I can't express my gratitude enough to all of my readers! To everyone who picked up P.S. JANE and gave her a chance, thank you! It means the world to me you took the time to dive into this super world. If you would be so kind to leave a review, that would bring me so much joy. Thank you for your support and kindness! <3

Also By Jessica Julien

A Spectacle of Souls

Rise of the Ringmaster (short story)

Christmas Donut

About the Author

Jessica Julien is a stay-at-home-mom, wife, co owner of a small bookish shop, and avid wanderluster. When not curating book boxes or folding laundry, she spends her time penning YA novels inspired by her love of all things dark and twisty.

She loves dark roast coffee, dark chocolate, watching The Office, and is obsessed with pumpkins, pie, and pandas. When the weather is right, she can be found road tripping with her husband, kids, and dogs.

Connect with Jessica on social media! She is most active on Instagram, but can also be found on TikTok, Facebook, and all the things. Search for @jessicaljulien to be friends!

www.ingramcontent.com/pod-product-compliance
Lightning Source LLC
Chambersburg PA
CBHW031456160726
47994CB00005B/2060